S0-ASF-315

Will Summer
find her one
true love?

The crush of her life . . .

Standing there was a tall, muscular, darkly handsome young guy. He looked as if he might be anywhere from eighteen to twenty-five years old, but Summer knew for a fact that he was only seventeen. She knew because, as impossible as it seemed, he was none other than Sean Valletti.

Sean Valletti, the crush of her life. The guy she'd drooled over since freshman year. The guy who'd broken her heart a thousand times without even noticing it.

"Are you from . . ." Sean began, looking at Summer in confusion. "You remind me of someone."

Someone you managed to look right through for the last three years, Summer thought. The invisible girl. "I'm Summer Smith," she said miserably. "You know, I sit behind you in—"

"Summer Smith?" Sean said incredulously. "No way." He looked her up and down with no attempt to be subtle. "You've been sitting behind me all year? Wow, I must have been blind."

Don't miss the other two books in this
new romantic trilogy:

#1 June Dreams
#2 July's Promise

Available from ARCHWAY Paperbacks

For orders other than by individual consumers, Archway
Books grants a discount on the purchase of **10 or more**
copies of single titles for special markets or premium use.
For further details, please write to the Vice-President of
Special Markets, Pocket Books, 1230 Avenue of the Americas,
New York, NY 10020.

For information on how individual consumers can place
orders, please write to Mail Order Department, Paramount
Publishing, 200 Old Tappan Road, Old Tappan, NJ 07675.

Summer

August Magic

Katherine Applegate

AN ARCHWAY PAPERBACK
Published by POCKET BOOKS
New York   London   Toronto   Sydney   Tokyo   Singapore

The sale of this book without its cover is unauthorized. If you purchased this book without a cover, you should be aware that it was reported to the publisher as "unsold and destroyed." Neither the author nor the publisher has received payment for the sale of this "stripped book."

This book is a work of fiction. Names, characters, places, and incidents are either products of the author's imagination or are used fictitiously. Any resemblance to actual events or locales or persons, living or dead, is entirely coincidental.

AN ARCHWAY PAPERBACK *Original*

An Archway Paperback published by
POCKET BOOKS, a division of Simon & Schuster Inc.
1230 Avenue of the Americas, New York, NY 10020

Produced by Daniel Weiss Associates, Inc., New York

Copyright © 1995 by Daniel Weiss Associates, Inc., and
Katherine Applegate

Cover art copyright © 1995 by Daniel Weiss Associates, Inc.

All rights reserved, including the right to reproduce
this book or portions thereof in any form whatsoever.
For information address Daniel Weiss Associates, Inc.,
33 West 17th Street, New York, NY 10011, or Pocket Books,
1230 Avenue of the Americas, New York, NY 10020.

ISBN: 0-671-51032-0

First Archway Paperback printing August 1995

10 9 8 7 6 5 4 3 2 1

AN ARCHWAY PAPERBACK and colophon are
registered trademarks of Simon & Schuster Inc.

Printed in the U.S.A.

IL 7+

For Michael

August Magic

1

All You Need Is Air, Water, Food, and . . . a Little Revenge.

Sunshine. Fresh air. Freedom. And the promise of clean water, real food, and soap. If Summer Smith had ever experienced a moment of transcendent, perfect happiness, it was right then, right as she was pulled from the clinging, dark moistness of the cave where she and Seth had been trapped for a harrowing night. She soaked in the blistering heat and blinding light of the tiny, remote island they'd chosen for a scuba-diving expedition the day before.

Summer could not open her eyes at all for several minutes while Marquez hugged her and J.T. hugged her and various unknown Coast Guard guys hugged her.

Finally she cautiously opened one eye and saw Marquez looking ratty but beautiful, and J.T. looking unusually shy.

"How are you guys?" Marquez asked.

"Great," Seth said. "Excellent. We'll really have to do this again someday, like when hell freezes over. By the way, did you guys see our boat?"

"No. The boat got loose. I hope it's insured," J.T. explained. "The Coast Guard says it got in the way of a tanker."

"So how did you find us? I mean, how did you even know we were here?" Summer asked.

"Marquez saw something come flying up out of the ground, right here," J.T. said, indicating the hole in the ground. "She said it looked like an arrow with a yellow snake attached. We were just getting ready to give up."

"The spear gun," Seth confirmed. "I fired it up through the hole in the top of the cave, with a rope attached."

"As for how we picked this particular island . . ." Marquez looked at J.T. He nodded, giving her his permission.

"What?" Summer asked. But even as she asked she felt a queasy sensation in the pit of her stomach. Some sixth sense warned her that she was not really ready for the answer.

"I thought maybe J.T. might have some instinct about the right place," Marquez said, fixing Summer with an intense stare.

"Actually, it turned out I didn't," J.T. said, grinning crookedly.

"But . . ." Marquez took a deep breath. "Look, I don't know if this is the right time to lay this on you, Summer, but I have an idea that . . . I mean, there're all these reasons to think that . . ." She looked to J.T. again.

J.T. looked down at the ground. "Summer, I think it's possible that I am . . . your brother. I think I may be Jonathan."

"Jona—" Summer tried to breathe and couldn't. *Jonathan? Alive?*

"It's just a theory," J.T. said.

But Summer could no longer hear him. The world was spinning around her, as if the tiny island were on some giant turntable. She heard several people call her name.

And then Summer fainted. Her eyes rolled up in her head. Her knees buckled. And she went down.

When she woke up she was in a large helicopter, strapped onto a stretcher, surrounded by a gallery of concerned faces.

"What?" Summer said, frowning.

"I said, you're awake!" Marquez yelled, making herself heard over the vibrating, thumping roar of the helicopter's engines.

"I know," Summer said. "I know when I'm awake. Why wouldn't I be?"

"Because you passed out," Marquez said.

"No way." Summer tried to sit up, couldn't, and looked down at the red webbing strap that went across her chest like a seat belt. "Oh. What happened?"

"It was very *Gone with the Wind!*" Marquez said, shouting to be heard. "You zoned. You went out."

"Here," Seth said. He was holding a canteen to her lips. "Water."

Summer took it in greedy mouthfuls, not an easy thing to manage since she was lying on her back. When she was done she smiled at Seth. "Excellent. Much better than trying to lick condensation."

"They have food too," Seth said, saying the word *food* the way very hungry people say it.

"Can I get unstrapped?" Summer asked the nearest Guardsman.

"Um, sure, I guess," he said. He unfastened the strap, and she sat up, gazing around the inside of the helicopter. It was very spare, just bare aluminum and big yellow-and-black warning signs advertising various dangerous things.

The door was partly open, letting in damp, superheated air, and through the opening she could look down and see the perfect blue-green waters of the Gulf of Mexico zipping by a hundred feet down. The sun blazed, as it usually did in these islands beyond the southernmost tip of Florida. It would have been a beautiful sight at any time, but at the moment it was even more moving, and almost as beautiful as the ham and cheese sandwich Seth handed her.

"Don't scarf it too fast," Seth advised, putting his lips to her ear so she could hear him. He wanted to be close to her, and she wanted him to be close too.

"Food," Summer said reverently between bites. "Food. Food is so good. Air and water and food,

4

that's all that matters. If you have air and water and food, you should just shut up and be happy."

"They'll have us back on Crab Claw Key in just a few minutes," Seth said. He leaned close again and stroked Summer's blond hair, now matted with dried salt and somewhat less than Vidal Sassoon clean.

Summer leaned into him, pressed her cheek against his warm, bare chest, and circled him with her free arm. She continued eating. "We made it," she said.

"Yeah. Thanks to Marquez and J.T. and the Coast Guard," Seth said, carefully including everyone.

Summer gave him a kiss that was partly flavored with mustard. He looked as if he wanted to continue the kiss, but Summer had her priorities, and priority number one was finishing the sandwich and moving on to the package of Hostess cream-filled cupcakes she'd spotted in the plastic bag the Coast Guard had provided.

And then it came back to her: J.T.

He was sitting a little back from the knot of bodies, leaning forward in a red webbing seat, watching her with an intense, prying, skeptical expression. He was looking past her, in a way, or through her.

Their eyes met. Summer's eyes were blue. So were J.T.'s. His hair, like hers, was blond. They certainly looked as if they could be brother and sister. But there were a lot of blue-eyed blonds in the world. They weren't all part of the Smith family of Bloomington, Minnesota.

And if he really was Jonathan . . . She felt as if she might faint again. Fainting might be easier than coming to grips with reality . . . if J.T. was Jonathan. If Jonathan was *alive*.

If J.T. really *was* Jonathan . . . The incredible hugeness of the idea hit her with sudden force. No wonder she'd fainted. It would mean so much. To her parents, and to his parents, who now would not really be his parents anymore, who might in fact be kidnappers.

"Mom and Dad," Summer whispered, lost in her own careening thoughts. How could she tell them? What could she tell them? This was impossible. She stared hard at J.T. Was this some kind of a joke? Was this his idea of funny?

Summer reached for the cupcakes and tore open the plastic. She was still hungry. But she got no pleasure from the food. Monumental, endless, unpredictable repercussions . . . Some people would come out feeling that their lives had suddenly changed for the better, and others might be destroyed.

J.T. must have been thinking much the same thing. He shrugged and made a worried who-knows face.

Summer met his gaze and tried for a reassuring smile that never formed. Are you my brother? she wondered. Are you Jonathan?

And in J.T.'s eyes, so like her own, she saw the

same question: Am I Jonathan? Am I your brother?

"What are we going to do?" Summer asked him.

"I don't know," J.T. admitted.

"My parents . . ." Summer let the thought hang there. J.T. understood.

"Yeah. Mine too. I mean, my folks, my . . . I think of them as my parents, you know?"

Seth cleared his throat tentatively. "Um, look, this is none of my business, but Summer has had a really bad time here. And so have I. And I think maybe this whole thing should be put on hold for a while. You know, let everyone get some sleep? You don't have to make any decisions right this minute."

Summer felt deep relief. Too much relief. She should not *want* to avoid reality. But she saw the same relief reflected in J.T.'s eyes.

"Maybe, yes," J.T. said, "maybe we'd better chill for a while. See what's what before we jump to any big conclusions."

"Yeah," Summer said. She still felt a little guilty. But the relief outweighed the guilt. There was plenty of time to examine this explosive possibility. Plenty of time.

Seth stroked her hair. Summer smiled at him. For many hours in the dark she had been unable to see his face clearly. It was a wonderful face.

She pulled him close till his ear was next to her lips. "I love you," she said.

"It wasn't just the cave?" he asked, serious as usual. "Maybe you just wanted me to die happy."

Summer started to kiss him. She didn't care if the Coast Guard guys grinned and Marquez rolled her eyes. But J.T. was still watching her, dissecting her with his eyes. So she gave Seth a brief kiss on his cheek and tried to remind herself that all she needed to be happy was air and water and food.

"Don't expect great photography," Diana Olan said self-consciously. "I'm not exactly Steven Spielberg."

Two Florida Department of Law Enforcement special agents were in the small, stuffy room with her. The one named Reynoso seemed to be in charge. He was a small, dark man with a close-trimmed mustache and hair that had retreated back from most of his forehead. Diana had forgotten the other agent's name.

"This isn't film school," Reynoso said gloomily. "Go ahead and hit it, Pete," he said to the other detective.

Now the name came back to her—Pete Wallace. Alan Reynoso and Pete Wallace. She should probably try to remember those names.

Wallace aimed a remote control at the television. The TV sat on an industrial-looking steel stand with a VCR underneath. Diana sat at a painted metal table between the two detectives, feeling totally out of place in her wraparound skirt and halter top. The cops were wearing what might have been the only two business suits within fifty miles of Crab Claw Key.

"I'm hoping for an Oscar nomination," Diana said.

The special agents said nothing. The tape started.

The picture on the TV screen was jerky, making sudden sharp lurches to the left and right. The color was poor, giving the tape a washed-out, faded look, like a colorized black-and-white movie.

"This is the front door of the Merricks' mansion," Diana narrated.

On the screen the door opened.

"That's Ross Merrick," Diana said, trying not to sound as hostile as she felt.

"I'm familiar with him," Wallace said dryly. "Most cops in the area are."

"Turn up the volume," Reynoso directed.

Wallace pressed a button on the remote, and Ross's leering tones filled the room. "Why, it's Diana. What a surprise. Come back to get more of what I started to give you?"

Diana intercepted a glance that went from Reynoso to Wallace. Reynoso cocked an eyebrow.

"This is the main entrance hall at the Merrick estate," Diana said. "It's very impressive."

"I could put my whole house in that hallway," Wallace said glumly.

The picture followed Ross, swinging back and forth as Diana walked. The camera had been concealed in a shoulder bag. She'd done what she could to keep it stable, but she hadn't wanted to alert anyone to what she was doing.

The next shot was of an unoccupied desk with

bookshelves behind it. At this point the picture grew less jerky, since she'd sat down and the camera was positioned on her knee.

"You could probably fast-forward through this part," Diana suggested.

Wallace did, stopping at the sudden arrival of another person in the room, a handsome, athletic, dark-haired young man with a very somber expression on his face.

"That's Adam," Diana said. "He's Ross's younger brother. He . . . he used to be my boyfriend."

Senator Merrick walked into the picture. Diana heard both cops shift in their seats. Wallace leaned forward, focusing intently.

"Well, let's hear it," the senator said. He glanced at his watch. "What's this about?"

"This is about rape." Diana heard the tremor in her own voice. At the time she had felt bold and fearless, but there had been fear in her tone. Maybe it was just distortion from the video camera.

"*Attempted* rape," Ross said.

Diana saw a slight, predatory smile on Wallace's face, quickly erased.

The conversation played as she remembered it, as she had seen it already on this same videotape. Ross, furious and contemptuous; Adam, sad and disturbed; the senator, barely containing his fury at his own son and the mess he'd created.

"This is the good part," Diana announced in a low voice.

On the TV screen Ross lost control and lunged at her. The picture went crazy, jerking wildly, focusing on the ceiling, on the floor, on the arm of the chair.

A crazy, sideways view of the senator came into focus. He swung hard and buried his fist in Ross's stomach. Ross collapsed on the floor.

Wallace whistled softly. "That had to hurt."

Even Reynoso seemed mildly impressed. "Huh," he said.

Diana's voice came next, a shrieking, enraged cry. "Now do you see? Do you see what he is? Do you see what your son is, Senator?"

The scene calmed somewhat. The picture showed Ross, only partly in the frame, crawling to a chair. It showed Adam comforting his father.

And then the senator delivered his ultimatum— if Diana ever accused Ross of anything, the senator would ruin her. He owned the prosecutor, he said. He controlled the local police. He would find a way to destroy Diana. Or . . . she could keep quiet and walk away with a large check.

"Oh, man," Wallace said, awestruck.

Diana realized that he and Reynoso were more stunned by this portion of the tape than by what had gone before.

The tape went on. The senator left. Adam walked her out to the front steps of the Merrick estate.

And then had come the strangest moment of all for Diana.

She'd been carrying a small tape recorder as well

as the video camera, wanting some backup, knowing she'd never get a second chance to do this.

Adam had spotted the tape recorder in the waistband of her slacks and had yanked it out. He'd listened to the recording and then, to Diana's amazement, he'd handed the tape back to her.

The picture on the TV screen went to gray fuzz. Wallace turned it off.

"I guess they aren't *all* rotten, huh?" Wallace said. "The kid, Adam, he seems all right."

"That did surprise me," Diana said softly. "He swore he'd never go against his family."

"Hell of a piece of work," Reynoso said, eyeing Diana with open respect.

"Can you . . . can you arrest Ross?" Diana asked.

Reynoso looked thoughtful. "There's nothing on there that is a straight confession. He never says, 'Look, I tried to rape you.'"

Diana felt panicky. "But . . . but isn't it obvious?"

"Obvious, yes. But is it evidence? That's another question. We can arrest Ross Merrick, but can we get to court? Can we convict? That's the next question. We have the tape, and we have your testimony."

Diana felt confused. She'd been certain that the tape was more than enough proof.

"Of course, Ross Merrick may choose to work out an arrangement for the sake of his father," Reynoso said.

Wallace nodded. "Yeah, I guess we'll see if the

family loyalty goes both ways. See whether he's going to leave his old man hanging out to dry."

"His old man? What? You mean the senator?" Diana asked. "Why would this involve him?"

Reynoso shook his head in amusement. "Don't you know what you have with this tape? It isn't a confession from Ross Merrick, but it *is* stone-cold proof that the senator threatened you and offered you a bribe to keep you from reporting a crime."

"Ms. Olan, you have one of the richest and most powerful men in America by the . . . Well, let's just say you have him," Wallace said. "You have him good."

2

Home, Strange Home

The stilt house seemed almost unbearably pretty. It brought tears to Summer's eyes. She had thought many times over the past day that she would never see it again.

It didn't look like much, perhaps. It was a shabby, wooden-sided bungalow built out over the water, raised on tall pilings and connected to the shore by a walkway. Frank the pelican was sitting on the railing, and as they approached he deposited a glob of bird poop on the wood.

"Home, sweet home," Summer said, laughing. She and Seth were finally alone after a Coast Guard doctor had pronounced them both fit to be released.

They had slipped around the side of the Olan house, hoping to avoid Diana and her mother, Mallory. As far as Summer knew, neither her cousin nor her aunt had heard anything about her misadventure, and she wanted to keep it that way. Aunt Mallory would almost certainly have told Summer's parents, and they would have yanked her back to Minnesota faster than the speed of light.

Summer didn't want to leave Crab Claw Key, not yet. Not anytime soon. In fact, she wondered if she'd ever want to leave. Seth was there for the rest of the summer, and J.T. lived there year-round. Two very powerful reasons for her to want to stay.

She had to figure out the truth about J.T. And Seth . . . She didn't even want to think about having to leave him when summer ended. She wasn't going to do anything to hurry that moment.

She squeezed his hand tightly.

They reached the door. Summer went inside. All was how she'd left it. Nothing had changed. The very normalcy of it all seemed odd. It *had* been only a little more than a day, but it felt as if days and weeks and lifetimes had passed. How could her bed still be made? How could there still be the odor of adhesive and paint from the work Seth had done fixing up the house? How could the same posters be on the walls, the same picture of her parents be sitting on the table beside her bed?

"Seems kind of alien, doesn't it?" Seth said, echoing her thoughts as he joined her.

"A bed. With actual sheets," Summer said. She went over to it and sat down. It seemed very soft. She stroked her pillowcase.

"You okay?" Seth asked.

Summer thought about the question before answering. "I guess so. I'm weirded out over this whole thing with J.T. You know?"

"I can kind of guess," Seth said. He sat beside her.

"Plus, I halfway feel like I'm still in that cave," Summer said. "Although the part that really sticks with me is the part *before* we found the cave. When we were down to just a few minutes of air . . ."

Summer took a very deep breath, filling her lungs to capacity. Seth did the same. Neither of them thought it was funny.

"Yeah. I don't think I'll forget that myself," Seth said grimly. "Later, though—" He brightened a little. "Well, that had its nice parts."

"Yes, it did." Summer took his hand and raised it to her lips, kissing the bruised knuckles and pressing the palm against her face. "I guess it shouldn't have taken that to get me to admit how much I love you. I mean, maybe actually being on the edge of death was not necessary."

Seth laughed. "In the future let's agree to avoid situations that involve dying. I'm totally opposed to dying."

"It's going to seem almost strange sleeping alone tonight," Summer said.

"I could—" Seth began.

Summer shoved him playfully. "No, you couldn't."

He made a face. "Anyway, I have to go tell Trent what happened to his boat. The Coast Guard towed it back in, but it's going to take some major work to repair."

"You'll fix it," Summer said. "You're good with your hands." She kissed him deeply. "And you're not so bad with your lips, either. Now go away. I need to brush my teeth six or eight times and take a hot bath and eat every single thing in the refrigerator. And then I'm just going to sleep."

Seth stood. "Okay, I'll go," he said reluctantly. "Do what you said—sleep. Try not to think about all this with J.T.," he advised. "You'll think better when you're rested and everything is back to normal again."

Summer nodded agreement. "The question is, can I go back to normal again?"

"I know it will work out," Seth said.

"Yeah?" Summer asked, unconvinced. "Suddenly my brother reappears in my life— maybe. I don't know how it can work out. Not for everyone. Not for J.T.'s parents." She started to say something else, then stopped herself.

"What?" Seth asked.

"Nothing, I guess. It's just . . . last night, when we were in the cave, I saw something. Some*one*. I know this is going to sound totally insane, but it was this little boy, dressed all in white. And I've seen this boy in my dreams lately. Only, this wasn't a dream. He was there, in the cave. I mean, *really* there."

Seth looked worried for her. "Do you think it means something?"

"I don't know," Summer admitted. "He was in my dreams, and then he appeared in the cave." She shrugged and shook her head dismissively. "I probably *was* dreaming."

"What did this little boy do?"

"I asked him who he was, and he said he didn't know. And then he took a little red ball he was holding and threw it up through the hole. The hole we escaped through."

"Summer?" Seth said. "You are creeping me out."

Summer laughed. "Okay, okay. It was just a dream. Forget about it."

Seth kissed her on the forehead. "Get some sleep. And no dreams, unless they're about me."

Marquez slept too. She and J.T. had been up all night searching for Summer and Seth, and she was exhausted. But after only four hours of slumber she woke, fully alert.

She looked at her clock. It said 10:47. But whether that was A.M. or P.M., she wasn't sure at first. She looked at the curtain drawn across the storefront window that was one wall of her room. No sunlight peeked around the edges. It was P.M.

She snapped on the lights, a series of shaded lamps positioned around her cavernous room. It had been an ice cream parlor many years ago. The chrome and Formica counter was still in place, with red vinyl-upholstered stools arrayed in front. Mirrored shelves covered the wall behind, once filled with banana split dishes and now piled with Marquez's colorful wardrobe of T-shirts, halter tops, shorts, and bathing suits. What had once been the hot fudge warmer now spilled over with panties. The countertop was loaded with dozens of spray paint cans and pots of vivid acrylics.

The other two walls were bare brick—or had begun as bare brick. Over the years Marquez had covered them from floor to ceiling with a huge, brilliant, confused, intricate mural of pictures and graffiti. A spray-painted palm tree filled one corner, roots spread across the cement floor, branches fanned across the ceiling. A stylized mural showed her own family's arrival in Florida in a fugitive rowboat from Cuba, complete with an infant Maria Esmeralda Marquez. A stunning sunset sprayed red and gold covered a field of graffitied names—from Keanu Reeves to Mario Cuomo; from Ms. Palmer, her eighth-grade history teacher, to Lloyd Cutler, the lawyer Marquez wanted to be like someday; from Kurt Cobain to Bob Marley. And then there were the other names: former boyfriends, school friends, family friends, her brothers, her parents— even the old man who thought he was Ernest Hemingway and swept the downtown sidewalks with an imaginary broom.

In the middle of the maze of names and images was a rough white rectangle—the place where she had painted over J.T.'s name.

Marquez knew she should go back to sleep. But she felt restless and agitated, as she sometimes did in the wake of disturbing dreams. She didn't remember anything specific from her dreams, just a feeling of certain vivid colors and shapes.

Marquez knew that if she was going to be awake she ought to go upstairs and take a shower, wash her hair, watch some TV with her mom and dad and brothers. Or at least put on some clothes. But she didn't feel like performing familiar rituals. She was fired up. She was jumpy. Her skin was crawling with electricity.

Marquez snapped her fingers and tossed her head in short, quick jerks. Music. That was the first thing.

Veruca Salt? No, too mellow. The Cranberries? No, way too mellow. No, something harder, something to fit her dangerous mood. Old Nirvana, maybe. She slid *Nevermind* into the CD player and hit Play.

She swept all the paint cans together and dumped them next to the wall, just below the blank white square. She realized she was breathing heavily, as if excited or exhausted, or maybe both. She was. Both. It happened sometimes, for no apparent reason, this sudden need to paint.

She snatched up a spray can and began shaking it, the rattling little ball a perfect counterpoint to the music pounding from the CD.

With quick strokes she directed the crimson spray against the white. As she did something came over Marquez, as it did from time to time. Her thinking, rationalizing mind simply went away for a while. Her brain became as blank as the patch of white. Her hands grabbed at paints, then threw them impatiently away and reached for some new color. The sweat began to run down her forehead, and her hair flew with each angry toss of her head. Fumes filled the room, barely controlled by the big exhaust fan that had been painted to look like a sunflower. Her eyes stung, the music pounded, her bare feet slipped on the concrete floor, and her hair and body were highlighted with careless reds and blues and golds. She dragged her ladder over, and her brushes and rags and sponges and every tool she had.

The music had long since stopped, the CD played out, when at last she was done. Hours had passed unnoticed. She stepped back to look at it— J.T. reborn. Huge letters, shaded for a 3-D effect so that they leaped out from the wall and picked up the glint of the mural sunset, each line woven through the entire tapestry of her walls by connections of color that insinuated themselves around each name, each picture.

The real J.T., as he was in her life: too much a part of the whole ever to be completely painted out again.

Marquez sat down on one of the red vinyl stools and hung her head. She cried, and in wiping away tears smeared new colors over her face—the same colors that made J.T.'s name. She had tried to paint him out. He was confusion and trouble, now more than ever.

When they'd started going out, he'd just been

the cute cook at work. Then the simple, fun-loving guy had grown complicated. He'd learned he was not the biological son of his parents, though they had never told him directly. And he'd begun to wonder who he was and where he fit in. In the midst of it all, he'd grown angry and depressed. Who knew how he would respond to all this about being Summer's brother Jonathan? Knowing J.T., it would not be a peaceful adjustment.

It had all been too much for Marquez. She wasn't interested in complications and emotional problems. She was determined to keep her life orderly. She had her plan—one more year of high school, and sure, during that time she could be free and have fun and party. But then, she had determined, a different life would begin—college, law school, then a brilliant career in law. It was laid out. She already had the grades and the SAT scores.

Sixteen years ago her family had landed penniless in the United States, and the USA had taken them in, given them a chance and a hope they'd never had in Cuba. The family was dedicated to making good on that hope. Marquez was not going to be the weak link. She was not going to be the flake, the failure.

She looked around the room. The clock showed it was after two in the morning. The room reeked of fresh paint. She herself smelled of paint and sweat.

She saw herself reflected in the mirrors behind the counter—her hair and face and arms covered with paint, so that she seemed just another wild image, a part of the incredible wall behind her, like one of those 3-D hologram pictures you could stare at and then, whoa, a girl appeared.

"Very nice, Marquez," she said aloud to her reflection. She was exhausted and angry with herself, as she usually was after working on the wall. "Just be sure when you go to Harvard you get a room with wallpaper."

3

You Meet the Most Interesting People When You Should Be Sleeping.

Lying back asleep, his chest and legs bare, his blond hair fanned out, his eyes closed but fluttering behind his eyelids, he swirled down and down, falling in a way that had once scared him but now seemed familiar. He was falling down that same whirlpool, landing in that same dusty corridor, sticky with cobwebs, dimly lit. He followed it, the way he always did, back through time, back and back, brushing the cobwebs aside.

He emerged in the grassy field again, smaller, as he always was in the dream. A tiny little boy, struck by how close the grass seemed, how near he was to the ground.

And there it was. The red ball.

And there she was. The sun. The bright ball of light that had begun to appear in his dream.

As he bent to pick up the ball, he noticed for the

first time that he was wearing shorts. White shorts. And a white shirt.

Summer lay on her side, a sheet pulled up to her neck, one foot sticking out, her blond hair fanned across the pillow. Her breathing grew thready and uncertain, as it did when she dreamed.

For a while she was on the plane, listening yet again to the woman tell her tale of the tarot cards.

"But look," Summer said to the woman, "I didn't meet *three* guys. It was four."

"No, no, no," the woman said, shaking her head. "Just three. The other one isn't yours. Pay attention."

And then Summer was no longer on the airplane. She was no longer anyplace she knew. She was standing in a field, beside a swing set, only not standing. She was floating.

And there before her was the little boy in white. He was just picking up a red ball.

"I know you," she said to the little boy.

It was then that for the first time in his dreams, the sun spoke to him. "I know you," the sun said.

He held the ball in his hand. "I don't know *you*," he said. "I can't. You aren't here yet."

"Oh," the sun said. "I don't like that ball."

He nodded. "I know. It's not the ball's fault, though."

"I guess not," the sun said. "But . . . don't throw it."

He knew the sun was right. He knew what

followed from throwing the ball. "I've tried not to," he said. "But what *was* has to *be*."

Summer wanted to reach out and stop him somehow, but she seemed not to have a body. She was just a warm circle of light.

The little boy threw the ball. It flew through the air and landed. It rolled and came to a stop by a fence.

"Don't chase it," she pleaded. She didn't know why, but she felt dread filling her up, dimming the golden light she cast, chilling the warmth.

"I have to. I always have to," the little boy said. "It's the way it happened. . . ."

". . . I have to chase it. Maybe then I can find the truth," he said. He smiled at the sun. The sun was worried, but she couldn't help. She wasn't really there. That much he knew. That she wasn't real . . . not yet.

"Who are you?" the sun asked.

"I don't know," he said. "That's why I have to chase the ball."

Summer watched, helpless, as he chased the ball to the fence. Beyond the low fence, on the other side, was a car. The car door was open, and sitting there, sad beyond endurance, was a woman. A man stood by the fence.

The little boy in white stopped at the fence. He picked up the ball.

"No," Summer whispered.

The man reached over the fence and lifted the boy up high over the fence.

In her mind, she heard the boy cry out in fear. And all the light was gone. She was no longer the sun, though she was still warm, a glowing circle of warmth, safe and secure. But she heard that echoing cry deep in her heart even as she emerged from darkness into a harsh light and heard for the first time her own shrill, tiny, newborn voice repeating her brother's wail.

Summer cried out.

Her cry woke her. Her pillow was soaked with tears.

"Oh, jeez," she moaned. "Stop eating before you go to bed, Summer."

That was how it had happened, Summer realized. Sixteen years ago. Jonathan had been in the playground at the day care center, playing with his favorite, chewed-up red ball. Then he had simply disappeared. Witnesses said they might have noticed a car parked by the fence. There might have been a man standing there. But no one could be sure.

Jonathan. J.T.? Had she really met him in her dream? Had any of it been real?

What kind of reality could you expect in a dream?

The night before, she'd been in the cave, with Seth sleeping beside her. She'd slept with her head resting on his chest, listening to the sound of his breathing. Now she felt so alone.

She hugged her pillow close. It just wasn't the

same. She felt abandoned, which she knew was dumb. She hated feeling abandoned. Hated it.

"I wish you were here, Seth," she whispered.

Diana had often had difficulty sleeping, especially during the past year—the year that had come to be defined by the incident with Ross. She'd often lain awake, thinking of death. It had become a ritual—recalling the attempted rape; recalling in excruciating detail the moment when she'd realized that Adam was betraying her to protect his brother; remembering the feelings of self-loathing that had eaten at her, driving her again and again into the deep hole she thought would one day become her final experience of life.

But on this night she was not lying awake for those reasons. Not that depression was so far away—she could still feel its evil, seductive contours close by, calling softly to her. Depression had lured her often, even before the incident with Ross. That had merely lowered her defenses, made her vulnerable. And even now Diana was not on the verge of becoming a giddy optimist. She was not, she thought wryly, about to be reborn as Summer. But she *had* flushed the carefully hoarded pills down the toilet, flushed away her safety net of suicide.

She was restless. At first she'd fallen asleep easily, but she'd awakened an hour later, alert. Since then she'd lain there, tossing the covers on or off, fluffing pillows, trying every sleeping position—her back, her side, her other side, facedown. None with any success.

She replayed the events of the day till they became as familiar as old *Simpsons* reruns. The trip to the police. Showing the video. The statement she'd dictated and signed. The realization that her actions had sent a weird thrill through everyone in the FDLE office, part awe, part anticipation. They'd asked her to speak to no one, to let them decide when to take action. But she had come away certain that they would take action. By the time she'd left, the number of FDLE personnel had tripled— men staring at her, not in the usual way at all, but as if she were some rare, dangerous animal.

It was interesting, being dangerous. It made her smile in the darkness. But at the same time she felt uneasy. Not afraid so much as vaguely nauseated.

"I'm not going to get any sleep, am I?" she muttered.

She answered her own question by climbing out of bed. She retrieved the gauzy white robe she'd left on her chair, slipped it on, and went to the sliding glass door that opened onto her private balcony.

The night air was warmer than the air-conditioning by at least ten degrees. It had to be close to eighty, with humidity so thick it sparkled in the air like steam.

She went to the railing and rested both her hands on the wood. The moon peeked around a drifting cumulus. Most of the sky was clear, starlight twinkling through the damp air. The water of the bay was calm, as it almost always was, just tiny ripples to reflect the moonlight. Across the bay was the other side of Crab Claw Key—a few porch lights shining here and there; someone who insisted on shining spotlights on a tall palm; and down near the point, the green light that marked the end of the Merricks' dock.

Suddenly Diana felt uncomfortable. She felt as if . . . as if she were being watched. She glanced toward the Merrick estate. Surely there was no way they could see her from that distance—

She heard a slight rustling in the bushes below. Diana peered through the gloom. "Hey, who's there?"

No answer for a moment. Then a less surreptitious movement, someone stepping back from the bushes, stepping into the moonlight on the lawn.

"Don't be scared, it's just me."

It took Diana a moment to place the voice. She'd only heard it once before. One meeting, every single detail of which had stayed fresh in her mind. "Diver?"

"Yeah. Sorry. I wasn't sneaking around or any-thing."

Diana considered this. If he wasn't sneaking around, what exactly was he doing? Her heart was pounding. Her throat was tight. If she didn't know better, if Diana had not known herself to be cool and removed and not even slightly interested in a flake like Diver . . . well, if she hadn't known all those things, she'd have thought she was excited to see him.

"Wait there, I'll come down," Diana said. "I don't want Mallory—my mother—to wake up."

"I could come up there," Diver said. His voice sounded strange, almost shaky. Probably just the strain of whispering.

"The door's locked downstairs," Diana said. "I'd have to come down to let you in, anyway."

"No problem," Diver said.

To Diana's amazement, he planted a foot on the trellis that covered the outside wall of the family room, climbed to the top, levered himself up onto the roof of the family room, and walked across the sloping Spanish tiles to a point just above her balcony.

He stood there above her, wearing, as always, nothing but a pair of trunks. Summer had told her Diver never wore anything more. When his original trunks had been ripped, Diana, Summer, and Marquez had gone shopping to buy him a more complete wardrobe, but by the time they'd returned, he'd bummed an old pair of Seth's trunks and now seemed to think all his needs were met.

And, in fact, looking at him now, arm and shoulder and chest outlined in moonlight, Diana could see no good reason why he should be wearing anything more than he was.

"Come on down," Diana said.

He squatted at the edge of the roof and jumped lightly down beside her.

Diana was suddenly very aware of the sheerness of her robe, and the way the humidity had made it cling here and there. She backed away a few feet, making it look like a natural desire to gaze off toward the open water at the bay's mouth.

Diver seemed content to let the silence stretch. Diana considered going inside, finding some less flagrant thing to wear. But then, Diver always said he wasn't interested in girls. That's what Summer reported, anyway. He said that girls would disturb his inner peace, his *wa*.

It would serve him right if she did disturb his *wa*. Having him this close by seemed to be disturbing *hers*.

"Summer's okay," Diver said after a while. "I thought I should tell you."

"What do you mean?"

"They found her."

"What do you mean? Was she lost?"

"Yes," he said.

Diana shook her head. Clearly this was supposed to mean something, but she didn't have the slightest idea what. And she was a little annoyed to be standing there discussing Summer.

"Then I'm glad they found her," Diana said, making a mental note to ask Summer what had been going on.

Silence fell again. But now Diana realized she'd moved closer to Diver, and the obscure agitation she'd felt lying in bed was worse. She felt irritated. She plucked at the front of her robe to keep it from clinging.

"You know, I think Summer is kind of into

Seth," Diana said. The words were out of her mouth several seconds before she began to think about them. "I mean . . ." Okay, now what *did* she mean?

"I like Seth," Diver said. "He's the one who gave me these." He pointed at his trunks.

"So you're not jealous?" Diana said, digging the hole deeper.

He looked at her blankly. Then a slow, dawning smile.

He was beautiful, Diana realized, feeling inexplicably demoralized by the realization.

"It's not that way with Summer," Diver said shyly.

"Yeah, I know," Diana said dismissively. "Girls disturb your *wa*." Beautiful eyes. Beautiful lips. Even his hands . . . she wouldn't mind holding his hand. The thought shocked her. Because it wasn't as if she was thinking with her usual casual detachment that she would like to hold his hand—no, it was as if she was suddenly entirely focused, with absolute intensity, on the single idea of touching him.

"Some more than others," Diver said.

"What?" Diana managed to ask.

"Some girls disturb me more than others," he clarified.

Diana struggled for just the right thing to say. Something clever but not too coy. Something normal-sounding, even though she was feeling distinctly abnormal. What she wanted to say was, What girl? Summer? Marquez? Me? Hillary Clinton? Did I mention me? What she did say was, "Uh-huh.

Yeah. I guess that would be true. So I guess you'd just want to stay away from that type of girl."

He nodded solemnly. "Yes." Then he grinned impishly. "I suppose you think I'm crazy, right?"

Diana started to mouth the properly polite response, but then she laughed. "Diver, I can't call anyone crazy. When it comes to crazy, I don't think you're even in my league."

He said nothing, just waited.

"You know what I used to do? Every night?" Diana asked. "Right inside there, in my bed?"

"No."

"I used to lie there and think about killing myself," she said. "So how's that for crazy?" She began tapping her fingers on the wooden railing. "I had these pills. I used to enjoy counting them, you know? As long as I had them, I felt safe, like in a way I could deal with everything because in the end—well, in the end, there was always the end."

She waited for him to say something. And when he remained silent, she sighed. Brilliant, Diana. Wonderful. By all means, spill your guts to this near stranger. Right now he's wondering how he got himself into this. Right now he's hoping you don't have a weapon.

"Maybe you'd better take off," Diana said bitterly. Why had she done this? Why had she dragged her problems out for display?

"I don't think that would be an end," Diver said, surprising her.

"What?"

"I think that killing yourself isn't a real end to whatever pain you have. I think . . . I guess I think you can't look at life as having a neat beginning and middle and end, like a book. If you felt bad and killed yourself, those bad feelings would just go on to someone else—your mother, your friends. That's not right. You have to take the bad things that happen to you and . . . I don't know, change them. Turn them into something else."

"How about turning them into revenge?" Diana asked. "That's my present plan. Do to them what they did to you."

Diver shrugged. "I don't know about that. I guess I never got that chance."

Diana looked at him closely. He was telling her something important about himself. She started to ask him, but stopped herself. "You know, if you ever wanted to tell anyone . . . talk to anyone . . . I mean, like I said, I'm not someone who can ever call anyone else crazy."

Diver nodded.

"I wouldn't disturb your *wa* or anything," Diana said, trying to lighten the mood.

Diver bit his lip and looked away. "Yes, you would." He faced her, solemn, even sad. He raised his hand and, with only the lightest touch, stroked her cheek.

"The other day, when I saw you . . . Afterward I went to Marquez's house with her," he said. "I thought maybe she would make me forget. She kissed me. But I didn't forget. I was waiting for you tonight. Down in the bushes. Hoping you'd come out on the balcony. I was wishing you could just *know* that I was there. That I was calling you."

Diana took his hand and held it pressed against her cheek. "I couldn't sleep. I guess I heard you." She closed her eyes and savored the touch of his hand.

"I have to go," Diver said.

"Yes. Me too. Thanks for coming by."

Diana let him leave, though breaking the contact caused an almost physical sensation of pain and loss. He'd revealed all he could for one night, Diana knew. And so had she.

4

Unknowns, Uncertains, and Unstables

Hi, Mom, it's me, Summer. Look, I have something very serious to tell you. Maybe you should sit down. This is going to be the biggest thing I have ever told you."

Summer wiped the steam off the bathroom mirror and looked at her reflection. Her reflection made a dissatisfied face at her and slowly shook her head.

"If I tell Mom she should sit down, she'll think I got pregnant or something," she told her reflection. "She'll reach through the phone and strangle me."

Summer flipped on the blow dryer, used it to evaporate the rest of the steam, and then started on her hair.

"Mom! Hey, guess what! You are never going to believe this. Jonathan isn't dead or anything. He may be right here. He's a cook."

She rolled her eyes. "*He's a cook?* Any other

irrelevant information you'd like to include?"

She hung the dryer on the hook and went into the main room. Her gaze fell on the framed picture of her parents that she kept on her nightstand. She sat on the edge of her unmade bed and held the picture in her hands. "Mom, I have to tell you something, and it's kind of major, so I'm just going to say it—Jonathan is alive, and I think I've found him." She sighed. "At least, *maybe* I have. So *maybe* you should be happy. *Maybe* you should get all excited and call Daddy and tell him that sixteen years of being sad are over. Maybe."

She replaced the picture on the nightstand.

"Yeah, right, Summer," she muttered. "Why not also tell them that *maybe* they won the lottery so they should both quit their jobs? Maybe they should think Jonathan is alive and then find out he isn't, so they can go through all that pain again."

There was a discreet knock at the door. Quiet as it was, it made Summer jump.

"Yes?"

"It's me." Diver's voice.

"Come in," she said, relieved.

He stuck his head in. "I thought I heard you talking to someone. I was just going to make some breakfast."

"No, I wasn't talking to anyone," Summer said. "Go ahead. Hey, I have some excellent juice in the fridge if you'd like some."

"Cool." He looked at her quizzically. "Talking to yourself, huh?"

"Yeah. I guess so." She smiled at him. "I'm going to lie out on the beach with Marquez, so take your time here."

"You're okay, right?" Diver asked. He was searching for the juice in the refrigerator.

"Mmm. Yes, *I'm* okay," she said thoughtfully. "I'm sort of like Typhoid Mary. You know, someone who has a disease, only it doesn't affect them but they give it to whoever they touch? And then whoever they give it to is sick?"

Diver had found the juice. Now he withdrew his hand gingerly. "Um, what disease? You didn't drink out of this bottle, right?"

Summer laughed softly. "Don't worry, Diver. This disease won't affect *you*. J.T., sure. And his parents, and my parents . . ."

She was silent for a moment while Diver poured and drank a glass of juice. She could just tell her parents what she knew, let them do all the checking. After all, they were parental units, and she was slightly too young to be taking on all the burdens of the world.

Only, it would devastate her parents. It would raise their hopes, and then, if it turned out not to be true, it would leave them feeling worse than ever.

Suddenly she jumped up. "No," she said decisively. "As a matter of fact, it isn't going to be *anyone's* problem. Not until I'm completely sure. Thanks for working it through with me, Diver."

"No problem," he said.

*   *   *

It was a bright, sunny day. It almost always was in the Florida Keys. Which did not change the fact that bright was still bright, and sunny was still sunny, and the heat was just as real for being almost constant.

Summer and Marquez were heading for the beach, wearing sandals and sunglasses and bathing suits—as common an outfit on Crab Claw Key as a business suit was in Manhattan or a down parka in Minnesota. It was strange, Summer reflected, how quickly she had become inured to the idea of walking around in public half naked all the time. The other day she'd gone into Burger King dressed in a bathing suit—not a thing one did back where she was from.

"I have a question," Summer said.

"What?"

"Is your butt painted green?"

Marquez stopped and twisted around to look. "Huh. Yes, it is."

"Any particular reason?" Summer asked.

"I was painting. I guess when I cleaned up I missed a spot." She resumed walking, but shot Summer a wicked grin. "Maybe later I'll ask Diver if he can come over and help me clean it off."

Summer wasn't buying it. Marquez was just trying to distract her. "What were you painting?"

"Stuff," Marquez said.

"Stuff like . . . *J.T.?*"

"Big deal. That doesn't mean anything," Marquez said unconvincingly. "I was just tired of that big, blank white spot on the wall."

"Right. I completely and totally believe you, Marquez."

"Oh, shut up," Marquez grumbled. "Besides, he's still seeing Lianne. It's not as if we're back together. And I need *someone* to go with me to the Bacch. J.T.'s with Lianne. Diver is with whatever weird, invisible spirit he's with."

"The what?"

"The Bacch. The McSween Bacchanal," Marquez explained to Summer. "What, you don't know about it? The party to end all parties? It's in five days. Jeez, do you live in a cave? It's this big street thing, like Mardi Gras, only no one speaks French. Lots of food, lots of drinks, lots of everything else you can think of. Music. Dancing. Vandalism. Guys peeing in alleyways. You know, pretty much the kind of good time you're used to back home in Blimpyburg, Iowasota."

"When are you going to stop making fun of Bloomington?" Summer asked grumpily. She hadn't slept all that well, and now, out in the heat, she felt groggy. First had come the strange, disturbing dream. And Diver had kept her awake, which was unusual. He slept on her roof deck, unless it was raining. Most nights she never even knew he was there. But the previous night he'd been humming some song for an hour. Very un-Diver-like. And then she'd spent the morning deciding just how many lives she should throw into turmoil. "So what are you saying? This is like some kind of local Mardi Gras?"

"Yeah, it's to celebrate the day when the guy who founded Crab Claw Key was hanged."

"Excuse me?"

"This guy named John Bonner McSween was some kind of pirate, and he used to have his boat here. But then the British Navy caught up with him and hanged him. So I guess before they finished him off he made some big speech about how he hoped they'd all have themselves a big party celebrating the fact that they'd got him at last. Anyway, that's the story. Every year it's a big thing."

"Like costumes and all?" Summer asked. They turned left, and the beach came into view at the end of a blessedly tree-shaded road. The trees framed a nice view at the far end of the street—a perfect, three-layered slice of crystal white sand, blue-green water, and pure, unclouded blue sky.

"It's not quite that organized," Marquez said. "Costumes would require actual planning. Mostly we're talking bathing suits."

"That's all people ever wear around here. This has to be the only place on earth where people wear shorts and halter tops to church."

"The important thing is, don't let them make you work that night," Marquez said. "They're going to try to get you to. But only total losers and married people work the night of the McSween Bacchanal."

"I guess I'll ask Seth what he's going to do," Summer said.

Marquez rolled her eyes. "Oh, so now you need his permission?"

They had reached the beach and were hotfooting around, looking for the perfect spot to spread their blanket. For Marquez, a perfect spot was usually defined as one with an easy view of good-looking guys playing volleyball.

"I don't need Seth's permission, but he and I are kind of boyfriend and girlfriend now," Summer said. "I mean, that's sort of official. Look, just put the blanket down already."

Marquez looked at her curiously as she unfolded the blanket. "What exactly went on between you two in that cave?"

Summer lay back and began spreading sunblock on her stomach. She had achieved a good tan and now didn't want to carry it too far. On Crab Claw Key the sun was out almost every day, and if she wasn't careful, she'd be a piece of leather by the time summer came to an end. Plus she didn't have Marquez's naturally dark skin.

"Nothing," Summer said. "I just kind of realized that I was being silly, keeping Seth at a distance."

"Uh-huh. So did you guys do it?"

"No!" Summer said, flustered, as she often was, by her friend's directness.

"You didn't?" Marquez seemed surprised. "You're stuck in a cave with a cute guy and only a few hours to live and you didn't even think to yourself, whoa, I don't want to die a virgin?"

"It didn't really come up," Summer said, tossing a handful of sugar white sand on Marquez's oiled back.

"Hey, stop that. Look, all I'm saying is that it would have been a pretty good excuse. Who's going to say you shouldn't just go for it under those circumstances?"

"The circumstances were that we were both scared and I hadn't brushed my teeth since that morning."

Marquez sighed. "Wait a minute. You're on death's doorstep, you're trapped with a very cute guy—even if he is a little too wholesome for me—and you don't do it because you think you might have bad breath?" She sighed again. "On second thought, maybe you *should* work the night of the Bacch."

"You're saying you would have done it?" Summer asked.

"Absolutely."

"Have you ever done it? Or are you just talking big, as usual?" Summer asked. She felt a little forward asking the question, but Marquez had goaded her.

"I've never been trapped in a cave," Marquez said defensively.

"Hah," Summer said.

"Oh, shut up. So if you didn't do it, why all this stuff about having to ask Seth's permission to go to the Bacchanal?"

"Did I say I had to ask his permission? No."

46

"But it's the big *L*, huh?" Marquez asked. "I mean, the *L* word was spoken out loud by both parties?"

Summer laughed. "The *L* word may have been spoken." She closed her eyes for a moment, savoring the memory. Yes, the *L* word had definitely been mentioned.

Marquez gave an exaggerated shudder. "That's too bad. Once the *L* word is out there, it's hard to ever take it back. Believe me, I know."

"Speaking of which . . . ," Summer began.

"Let's not change the subject. We're discussing your messed-up love life, not mine," Marquez said. "All I'm saying is this whole love thing is like . . . what's that disease? The one you get from mosquitoes, and it keeps coming back?"

"Encephalitis?"

"No. The other one."

"Malaria."

"Like malaria, right. Once you have the fever it can just come back all of a sudden, making you hot and feverish and delirious." Marquez panted theatrically. "Anyway, I'm just telling you, once you start saying the *L* word, it isn't easy to take it back."

"Maybe I don't want to take it back," Summer said. Everything was bright red beneath her closed eyes. She scrunched her eyelids tighter and got nice dark blue explosions. "I do love him."

"Yeah? That's what you think now," Marquez said. "But I have one word for you. One very important word."

Summer waited, but naturally Marquez outwaited her. "All right, what word?" Summer demanded, opening her eyes. "Jeez, make me beg already."

"The word is . . . *August.*"

"August. Okay. That clears everything up," Summer said dryly.

"Laugh all you want. People always forget August when they come down here for the summer. And you may have noticed that as of today, it's August. And after August?"

"Call me crazy, but I have to say . . . September?"

"Exactly. June is fine. July is fine. But August is upon us, and you're on the downside of summer, Summer. At the end of the month all you tourists fly off in different directions. You go back to Billybobtown, and Seth goes off to whatever pathetic, repressed midwestern cemetery he's from."

"Eau Claire, Wisconsin," Summer said automatically.

"Exactly. Ear Clean, Wisconosa. I knew that." Marquez grinned, hugely amused by herself.

But Summer wasn't. Billybobtown and Ear Clean were not a million miles apart. But they were not the same place, either. Not the same schools. Not the same lives.

And another thought had just appeared in Summer's mind—Marquez was still in love with J.T. That wasn't news. Summer had realized that long ago. But if J.T. really was Jonathan . . .

"Marquez?" she said. "Are you going to try to get back together with J.T.?"

48

"No. Absolutely not. But I think maybe I am going to let him get back together with me," Marquez said. "And I hope it's before the Bacch, unless I can get Diver to go with me, which seems unlikely."

When Summer didn't laugh, Marquez turned to peer at her from beneath shaded brows. "What?" she demanded. "What's the serious look all about?"

Summer shrugged. "It's just— What if J.T. really is my brother?"

"I give up. What if?"

"Nothing, I guess," Summer said. "Only, I was wondering whether he would stay here, or maybe go to Minnesota."

Marquez's smile disappeared. "I guess he would want to meet your—his—parents," she said slowly. "But that doesn't mean he'd live there."

"I guess you're right," Summer said.

"Of course I am," Marquez said confidently. "What kind of an idiot would deliberately choose Bloomington, Minnesota, over Crab Claw Key, Florida?"

Summer laughed along in agreement, and would almost have believed Marquez felt as sure as she sounded. Only, Marquez had never before actually said "Bloomington, Minnesota" without making a joke.

When Summer got home from the beach, the phone was ringing. To her surprise, it was Marquez. Summer had left her only twenty minutes earlier.

"Hey, Summer. Babe. What's been going on in your life since we got together last?" Marquez asked.

"I walked home. Then I picked up the phone. There, now you're up to date," Summer said. She squeezed the phone against her ear with her shoulder and glanced around the room. The stilt house wasn't always perfectly private—Diver occasionally appeared with very little announcement through the hatch in the floor.

"I got a call from work. They have a catering thing on board some big boat that just pulled in. They need a couple of waitresses who aren't doing anything tonight."

"But I *am* doing something tonight," Summer said. "I'm going out with Seth."

"You can go out with Seth any night," Marquez argued. "We'd split fifteen percent of the total food bill, so right there we'll probably make fifty each. Last summer when I did things like this, the boat guys always tipped extra. Last time the guy gave each waitress a hundred-dollar bill."

"Whoa."

"Yeah, whoa."

"Okay, I'm there. I'll just call and tell Seth."

Summer hung up the phone. She dialed Seth's number. He wasn't home, so she left a message on his answering machine. "Hi, it's me. Listen, I have to work tonight, but maybe we could get together afterward, if you still feel like it." She almost hung up the phone, but then remembered that Seth lived with his grandfather. "I'll miss you, little fuzzy wuzzy bunny," Summer said, choking down her own laughter. "Wittle Summer wuvs you." She hung up the phone, well satisfied by the image of Seth playing the message back with his grandfather listening.

"Jeez, I'm spending too much time with Marquez," Summer muttered.

At seven o'clock Summer arrived at the Crab 'n' Conch, wearing a pair of white shorts and a matching white halter top. Uniforms were not required on jobs outside the restaurant, and she knew that it would be hot work, at least until the sun set.

Marquez was already there, folding linen napkins in a corner of the kitchen. She was wearing a pair of shorts too, though hers were several degrees less modest than Summer's, and a brightly patterned bikini top. The usual evening rush was going on around them, waitresses hurrying in and out shouting orders, dishwashers clattering plates, cooks cursing and sweating in the intense heat.

J.T. was down on one end of the line, assembling the food for the private party. He was preoccupied and busy, but when Summer arrived he glanced up and sent her a smile.

"Hi," Summer said.

"Hi. You look great. In fact, normally I'd make some clever, flirtatious remark." He shook his head in bemusement. "I guess that would be in pretty bad taste now."

51

"I don't know," Summer admitted. "I guess so."

J.T. returned to arranging little finger foods on a long steel tray. "I don't exactly know what to do now, about all that stuff."

"Me neither," Summer said. "I mean, we should try to figure out whether it's true or not."

"I thought the same thing. First of all, what are the odds? We can't just screw up everyone's lives without being sure. But how do we be sure, exactly?" he asked. "I mean, what are we going to do? Compare blood tests?"

Summer shook her head. "I don't know. I just know I don't want to get my parents all excited and then find out it isn't true."

"I agree," he said solemnly. "And there's something else too. Whatever the truth is, I can't get my folks in trouble."

"Trouble? Why would they be in trouble?" Summer asked.

J.T. met her gaze with eyes so like her own. "Look, someone is going to want some explanation for how I came to be J.T. instead of Jonathan."

"Wow, I hadn't even really thought about that," Summer lied, suddenly feeling overwhelmed.

"I have," J.T. said solemnly. "It's about all I can think of." Summer saw his gaze dart toward Marquez. She was flirting ostentatiously with Alec, the bartender, who was by the sink cutting lemons.

"Are you going with us to this thing?" Summer asked.

"Yep. I'm handling the food. So you're stuck

with me tonight." J.T. grinned. "And we're both stuck with her." He jerked his head at Marquez.

"We'll figure everything out, J.T.," Summer said reassuringly. She took his hand, which was greasy with crabmeat stuffing. For some reason she felt like crying. What if? The question never seemed to be far away from her thoughts. What if?

"Yeah, of course we will," J.T. said.

"Honestly, J.T., I can't leave you alone for five minutes." It was Lianne, bustling back into the kitchen with a full tray of dirty dishes. She set the tray down and took J.T.'s hand from Summer. "Summer, I'm disappointed in you. I expect Marquez to be trying to steal other people's boyfriends."

Lianne's voice was only mock angry, but in the reference to Marquez there was genuine resentment. Lianne stretched up on her toes to kiss J.T. on the lips. Summer found the moment strangely embarrassing. Marquez obviously wasn't pleased either.

"Lianne," Marquez said, leaving the bartender's side, "I'm surprised to see you here. I heard that you joined the circus as the two-faced woman."

"That's funny," Lianne shot back. "I heard the same thing about you, only it was as part of the elephant act."

"I guess everything looks big when you're a midget," Marquez said.

"Excuse me," J.T. interrupted, "but we all have work to do, right?"

"Well, I'd love to go on trading insults with you, Marquez, you're such an easy target," Lianne said, "but I have to get changed."

"Finally getting that plastic surgery?" Marquez said gleefully.

"No. I'm going with all of you. They just called in to say they're adding guests, which means an extra waitress."

5

Revenge in Different Degrees of Purity

The cabin cruiser was long, and not a particularly elegant-looking boat, but definitely large. Larger than a Greyhound bus, and brightly lit with red Japanese lanterns hung on lines that drooped from the mast to the bow and from the radar dish to the stern.

Summer, Marquez, Lianne, J.T., and Alec the bartender all arrived on time, just as the sun was dipping toward the cooling waters of the Gulf of Mexico.

"Nice little raft, isn't it?" Marquez remarked dryly. "Someday I'm going to own one of these, only not so tiny and cramped." Marquez and Summer helped set up the buffet inside the carpeted and wood-paneled main cabin, which opened out onto the broad stern deck, where most of the party was to take place.

J.T. was nearby, lighting little cans of Sterno under the steel chafing dishes on a side table and shuttling back and forth to the galley, which was down a short set of three steps.

"Has anyone seen the guy who owns the boat?" Lianne asked, coming up with a box of paper napkins.

"No," Summer said. "Why?"

Lianne shrugged. "Nice to know who we're working for."

"Some fat, rich old guy with a hairy back, little stick legs, and pinkie rings," Marquez muttered under her breath. "That's what they always are. He'll drink Crown Royal, and after he's had two or three he'll start asking me if I like older men."

J.T. laughed. "The world according to Marquez."

"Marquez, why are you so cynical?" Lianne asked petulantly, seemingly annoyed that J.T. had laughed.

"Why am I cynical?" Marquez asked. "Because it works. Anytime you want to try to figure out why someone is doing something, just apply the most cynical interpretation you can come up with, and you'll be right about ninety percent of the time."

Lianne shook her head in disgust. "You should be a politician or a lawyer when you grow up. *If* you grow up."

Marquez laughed delightedly. "Exactly! That's just what I plan to be—a lawyer."

J.T. snorted derisively. He winked at Summer,

who was drinking a glass of soda and trying to stay out of what looked like a brewing fight. "Marquez a lawyer. And I might become a transvestite pygmy rabbit jockey," J.T. said.

This struck Summer as so funny that she choked on her soda. But Marquez didn't think it was at all funny. "See, that's why you and me are no longer you and me, J.T.," she said. "You have no faith in me."

J.T.'s eyes flashed. "Bull, Marquez. You're the one who doesn't have faith. Lawyer. Jeez, give me a break. You're the only person who knows you who is dumb enough to believe that."

"Now you're calling me stupid?" Marquez demanded.

Summer noticed that Lianne was content to stand by and watch, smugly pleased at this new evidence of the permanent rift between her new boyfriend and his old girlfriend.

"No, I'm not calling you stupid," J.T. said angrily. Then, much more softly, "I'm calling you an artist."

Marquez started to say something angry, but hesitated, looking confused.

Lianne seemed to realize that the conversation had taken a dangerous turn. "I think Marquez should be whatever she wants to be," she said, suddenly Marquez's defender.

"It isn't a question of what she should be someday." J.T.'s look was just for Marquez. "It's a case of what she is right now. She's an artist. She'll always be an artist. Send her to Harvard, or put her in a little gray business outfit and stick a briefcase in her hand, and she'll still be an artist." He returned his attention to a Sterno pot that would not catch fire.

Marquez busied herself with her work, viciously slicing limes into little wedges. Summer watched her, recalling the awed, overwhelmed feeling she'd experienced when she first went into Marquez's room. J.T. was right—Marquez was an artist. It bothered Summer a little that she hadn't seen it clearly before. It made her a little jealous of Marquez. It would be nice to *be* something, to be so precisely identified. Although evidently Marquez didn't think it was so great.

Then Summer shifted her gaze to J.T., and once again she experienced the queasy feeling that he represented change on a scale so massive it was impossible to grasp. What would her parents think of him? Would her mother—*their* mother, perhaps—be proud of the way he had grown up?

Summer saw Marquez jerk her head toward the gangway, a warning. Someone was coming aboard from the pier.

It was a man in his sixties, carrying a cocktail glass. He was fat, with a huge stomach hanging over his shorts. From the bottom of the shorts extended two narrow stick legs. His bare chest and back were matted with white and gray hair. Summer peered closely at his hands. Yes, there was a pinkie ring.

Marquez arched an eyebrow and grinned cockily.

Summer looked at J.T. "Just like she described," she said under her breath.

"Oh, yeah?" Lianne said. "Well, she didn't predict *him*."

Summer looked back, and there, emerging from behind the wide, waddling form of the man, was a tall, muscular, darkly handsome young guy. He looked as if he might be anywhere from eighteen to twenty-five years old. But, as it happened, Summer knew for a fact that he was only seventeen.

She knew for a fact how old he was because, as impossible as it seemed to her as she stood gaping with open mouth, her forgotten knife falling from her hand, he was none other than Sean Valletti.

Sean Valletti, the crush of her life. The guy she'd drooled over since freshman year. The guy who'd broken her heart a thousand times without even noticing it.

"Ah, good, good, you're here already," the man with the pinkie ring said.

"All set up," J.T. affirmed. "Are you Mr. Holland?"

"Dex Holland," the man said, extending a chubby hand to J.T. "And this here is my nephew. Just came down from Minnesota."

"Minnesota?" Marquez said. She gave Sean a good, long look in her inevitably provocative way, being even more blatant than usual in hopes of annoying J.T. She turned to Summer. "I didn't know they grew them this cute in Minnesota. Why did you ever leave?"

Summer could feel the blush crawling up her neck. It would have been nice if Marquez had just, for once, kept her mouth shut.

"Are you from . . ." Sean began, looking at Summer in confusion. He paused and tilted his head. "You remind me of someone."

Someone you managed to look right through for the last three years, Summer thought. The invisible girl. "Yes. I, uh, I mean, you do know me. I guess. Or not. I mean, I know you, anyway."

"You two actually know each other?" Marquez said.

"I don't think I do," Sean said.

"I'm Summer Smith," Summer said miserably. "You know, I sit behind you in—"

"Summer Smith?" Sean said incredulously. "No way." He looked her up and down with no attempt to be subtle. He smiled. "You've been sitting behind me all year? Wow, I must have been blind."

"Diana, someone is here to see you."

Her mother's voice rose up the stairs, a too-coy tone that affected Diana like fingernails on a chalkboard. But then a thought occurred to her. Diver? Could it be Diver?

No, that was ridiculous. Diver wouldn't just come up, knock on the front door, and announce himself to her mother. Diana smiled. No, that wasn't Diver's style.

"*Diana*. Do you hear me?"

"Unfortunately, yes," Diana muttered. She

turned off the TV. She had been reorganizing her room, moving things here and there, piling up clothing and possessions she no longer wanted. Too much of it held memories of sadder times.

She sighed and got to her feet. "Coming!" she yelled. But by the time she had risen completely and turned, he was standing there in the doorway.

"Adam!" she said, surprised and even a little frightened. "What are you doing here?"

Adam Merrick had always seemed to be surrounded by some kind of magnetic field that created in other guys a desire to like him and in girls a desire, period. He was tall and powerfully built without seeming at all ungainly. His dark hair was expensively cut, designed to look ever so casual. In all the time she had gone out with him, Diana had seldom seen him emotional or out of control. So it was a particular shock to see that his eyes were red, as if he had been crying. There was an odd, ashen color beneath the perpetual tan.

"Damn you, Diana," he said.

Diana recoiled. Before she could form a coherent response, he was in her room, closing the door behind him with a slam.

"I understood your going after Ross," he said. He was pointing his finger at her, trembling with barely controlled rage. "I understood that. Ross is dangerous. He's out of control. But my father? What's my father ever done to hurt you?"

"Get out of here, Adam," Diana said. Her voice sounded firm enough, but she was quivering inside.

Not so much from fear—Adam was not the type to become violent—but from the realization that it had all truly begun.

"No way, Diana. I want an answer. I *let* you keep that tape recorder, you know I did. I could have stopped you, but I let it go because I know Ross needs help, and I know he won't get it until someone shakes him up real badly. But my dad wasn't part of the deal."

"What's happened?" Diana asked, taking a deep breath to steady herself.

Adam snorted. "Like you don't know."

"They never told me what they were going to do," Diana said.

"No, you just put the knife in their hands, and however they decide to stick it in, well, that's not your problem, right?" The muscles in his jaw were in spasm. "They were just at the house, questioning him. Questioning my father. They told him to get a lawyer. I was there. He was . . . he couldn't look at me. My dad, he couldn't even look at me, and those idiots in their cheap suits smirking the whole time, pretending to be so respectful but practically drooling like a pack of hungry dogs."

Diana felt a knot tightening in her stomach. "And where was Ross?" she asked.

The question seemed to stun Adam momentarily. "Ross?"

"Yes. Where was Ross during all this?"

Adam looked away. His brow was furrowed. "He wasn't there."

"Hiding like the gutless little worm he is," Diana snapped.

But Adam wasn't really listening. "My dad sitting there having to listen to . . . these creeps, these Kmart cops cross-examining him. 'No, sir, we are not prepared to make an arrest at this time. But you need to get in touch with your lawyer, Senator. And don't leave the state of Florida, see, or otherwise it could be a matter for the FBI.'"

"I didn't want this to come down on your father," Diana said honestly. "It's Ross I want to see behind bars."

"Well, your little revenge is really all that counts," Adam sneered. "It doesn't matter to you that you're ruining a great man's life. Do you know what the media will do with this? Do you have any clue as to the kind of— You have to stop this," he said. He looked at her, threatening, blaming, pleading all at once. "You have to put an end to this."

"It's too late," Diana said. She felt her fear receding. Anger was returning, clean, strengthening anger. "You could have dealt with it a year ago, but the mighty Merricks always protect their own."

"That's something you'd better remember," Adam snapped. "We *do* protect our own."

There was scorn in Diana's laugh. "Really? How well did you and Ross protect your father?"

The shot went straight home. Adam seemed to crumple. Diana pressed on, noticing Adam's stricken look and not caring one bit. No more than Ross had cared for her that night when he'd slapped her and torn at her clothing and laughed at her cries for help. No more than Adam had really cared when he'd made his choice between his girlfriend and his brother.

"So the senator is in trouble?" Diana demanded. "Tough luck. I don't care. I don't give a damn. He threatened to ruin me if I charged Ross, right? Now look who's ruined. He threatened to make me look pathetic? Now who looks pathetic? You do, Adam, that's who."

"It's my fault," Adam said. "I should never have let you keep that tape. I was weak. I looked at you and remembered the way it was when we were together. I was stupid."

Diana shook her head. "It wasn't the tape recorder, Adam. It wouldn't have mattered if you had kept it. See, I had Summer's video camera in my bag. I figured you might find one or the other, but not both. Besides, my sweet mother burned the little tape. She's against me in this, but I don't even care."

Adam stared at her in amazement. "Well, you cold, calculating little witch." He laughed bitterly. "Don't count us out just yet," he said, but without much conviction.

"I know. You're very rich and very powerful, blah, blah, and you always protect your own, blah, blah, blah. But you know what? Pretty soon everyone in the country is going to know that Ross Merrick is a rapist, and law-and-order Senator Merrick covered up his crimes."

Adam was silent, staring at her with a weird, sideways look. Disbelief. Shock. "I don't even know you anymore, Diana," he said. "I don't even know what you've become."

"I guess you're right, Adam," Diana agreed. "You don't know me anymore. See, you used to recognize me better when I had the word *victim* tattooed on my forehead. You liked me that way. Diana the victim. Diana the depressed. Poor, screwed-up Diana. Go ahead, dump on Diana, she won't even know the difference."

Diana nodded thoughtfully, and even smiled. "That's okay. I understand why you treated me like crap, Adam. I treated myself like crap. I blamed myself. I turned it all inward. And to be honest, I got off on it in a way. In some sick way I enjoyed it, all the thoughts of suicide, all the drama of being the poor little victim. See, that's the beauty of depression, that's why it works. Because it seduces you. You start by *being* a victim, and then you begin *thinking* of yourself as a victim, *defining* yourself as a victim, and pretty soon you're a double victim, because now you're a victim of the feeling of being a victim. It's a spiral that sucks you further and further down."

"That's a great little speech," Adam said derisively. "Very Oprah. But now it's just about revenge."

"Justice," Diana said.

"Revenge. You just want to hurt the people who you think hurt you. Don't dress it up, Diana, it's just revenge."

65

Diana laughed, surprising both of them. "You're right, Adam. It is just revenge. And you know what? It's just like they say. Revenge really *is* sweet."

"I won't let this destroy my father," Adam said.

"I don't think that's up to you," Diana said. "It's up to Ross. All he has to do is confess. After that, no one will go after your father anymore."

Adam fell silent again. He nodded, a slight, unconscious movement. He knew she was right. If Ross confessed, that would probably be the end of it. "You have a videotape?" Adam said.

"The police have it now, at least one copy of it," Diana said.

"I—I know I don't have any right to ask you anything," he said. "It's just that if you give that tape to the media or anything, my dad . . . He's a proud guy, you know. Proud. To be on TV, with that tape making him look like a fool . . . I mean, okay, I know Ross has to be stopped. I'm just asking—I'm *begging* you. He's a great man. He has a position in the world. . . ."

"I'm not going to give the tape to anyone," Diana said, annoyed at herself for being moved by Adam's plea. But then, whatever else might be wrong with the Merrick family, there was genuine love between Adam and his father. Love and admiration of a degree that had always made Diana a little jealous. "I'm not going to give the tape to some sleazy tabloid show or anything," she promised. "I don't want to humiliate anyone.

I just want Ross not to be able to hurt anyone else."

"Thanks for that," Adam said, sagging with relief. "Thanks."

"Adam, we both know Ross is dangerous," Diana said. "I have to stop him. Call it revenge if you want. You know it has to be done. Your problem isn't with me. It's with your brother."

6

Summer Is a Very Bad Girl
but a Good Sister.

The party lasted the better part of five hours. Five hours of serving food and emptying ashtrays, and, as Marquez had predicted, dodging a few drunken come-ons. But through it all, Summer focused on one overarching fact—Sean Valletti was there. He was there on Crab Claw Key, and he had not missed a single opportunity all night to talk to her, to compliment her, even to help her carry more ice aboard from the pier. When she had spilled a drink and one of the old ladies had started giving her a hard time, Sean had intervened, forcefully defending Summer. And it seemed, though she might just be imagining it, that his gaze was never far from her.

Summer suspected he was interested in her.

This suspicion was heightened when Marquez said, "Jeez, he's panting around after you."

"Who?" Summer asked innocently. They were taking a brief coffee break, hiding in the dark on the seaward side of the boat, letting Lianne do all the work for a while.

"Oh, please. Even *you* aren't that much of a little Sunday school girl, Summer," Marquez said. "I'm talking about Mr. Complexion over there. Mr. Legs. Mr. Upper-Body Strength. Sean what's his name."

"Valletti. Sean Valletti." Summer grinned coyly. "He does have nice legs, doesn't he?"

"He has better legs than I have," Marquez said, "which I wouldn't mind, if he at least had the good taste to be interested in me, but apparently he is attracted only to his own kind—milk-fed midwestern virginal types."

"Well, I'm not interested in *him,*" Summer said, a little too strongly.

"Nooooo, of course not. Although I did see your jaw drop when you first saw him."

"I was surprised. I mean, I know him. I was surprised that he would be here, of all places."

"You two have anything going on back in Cheeseville?" Marquez asked.

"Not really," Summer said. "Although, to tell you the truth, I did always kind of think he was cute. For a while I had sort of a crush on him." She forced a laugh. "It was nothing. I get crushes on lots of guys. For a while I had this weird crush on the Vulcan guy on *Star Trek Voyager,* and I don't even watch the show."

70

"So, cutting through the crap, you were basically slobbering after this Sean guy, writing his name and your name together in hearts, trying out the sound of the name *Summer Valletti*—or maybe, being a good feminist, it was *Summer Smith-Valletti*—and kissing your pillow at night, wishing it were him."

"You know, Marquez, sometimes you get on my nerves," Summer said, annoyed at the total accuracy of Marquez's guesses.

"Oh, hi, there you are."

It was him. He had sneaked up from the far side, coming around from the bow. Summer jumped and blushed furiously, hoping and praying that he hadn't heard the last few seconds of their conversation.

"Guess I'd better go help Lianne clean up," Marquez said, batting her eyelashes at Summer and making a suggestive little kissy-kissy mouth that made Summer want to push her over the side of the boat.

"I should probably go too," Summer said, making no move to follow Marquez.

"Don't go," Sean said quickly. "You've been busy all night. The other two can handle it. Just about everyone's gone, anyway."

He was standing unnaturally close, and Summer held her Pepsi in front of her like a shield. "Did everything go okay?" she asked, at a loss for any more substantial conversation. "I mean, was the service all right? Did everyone get enough crab puffs?"

71

Did everyone get enough crab puffs? Yes, this was what she had waited three years to ask Sean Valletti.

"Who cares?" he asked, laughing.

"Well, it's my job," Summer said lamely.

"Don't worry. I told my uncle to be sure to give you a really big tip." He winked at her.

"Oh, that's okay," Summer said. "I mean, that's good, because the others like tips, but I don't really, you know . . . I mean, it's okay. You don't have to have him give us anything special."

Shut up now, Summer ordered herself. If she managed to babble until Marquez and Lianne missed out on a nice tip, they would take turns killing her.

"Can you believe this? Your running into me here?" Sean said.

"What are the odds?" Summer agreed.

"You know, I just can't believe we never went out," he said.

"We didn't," Summer said. "I'm pretty sure I'd remember."

"I know you would," he said. "Me too. I'd remember. You always just seemed like . . . like this girl, you know?"

"Uh-huh," she said, nodding agreement although she was entirely perplexed.

"Just this girl who was there and all," Sean clarified. "Then, when I saw you here, you were this *girl*." He looked at her appreciatively. "You're a babe. I hope you don't mind my saying that."

A babe. Sean Valletti had just called her a babe.

"I guess I don't mind," Summer said, gulping her drink and coming up with nothing but ice cubes. On the one hand, the phrase "a babe" was like some throwback. On the other hand, what did it matter what words he used? The point was, he had suddenly, amazingly, noticed her.

It could only be her carefully nurtured tan.

"So, when can we get together?" he asked. "You're staying here, right? I mean, all summer? All summer, Summer," he added, delighted by his wit.

"Um, sure, I'm here all summer," she said.

"Where are you staying?" he asked.

"I have this . . . this house. It's hard to describe."

"A house? By yourself? You have your own place?" he asked eagerly.

"Kind of." If you didn't count the guy who lived on her roof and used her bathroom and kitchen.

Sean grinned, showing a perfect smile. "Cool. So, how about this big festival thing they do here, this Botchanail?"

"The Bacchanal?"

"Yeah. I hear it's a major party. You and me? Are we there?" he asked.

"I, I, I, um, I, I, uh, see, I have this . . . I have to see if I can get off work," Summer babbled.

"Try real hard," Sean said. He took Summer's drink from her hand and tossed it into the water. He leaned close, too close by far, and before Summer could object, and before she could decide if she was even considering objecting, he kissed her lightly on the mouth.

73

Summer practically ran below deck, her head spinning. Standing there waiting for her was Marquez, a giant smirk on her face. Somehow Marquez had managed to help Lianne with the cleanup and still witness everything.

"Boy, Summer," Marquez said. "I mention the problem of the end of summer, and darned if you don't go right out and solve it."

It was a long walk home from the marina, and Summer was not looking forward to the trip in the dark. Marquez had walked from her own home, which was much closer. Summer had planned to go over to see Seth after work, since he lived just down the block from Marquez. But now she felt too tired.

Too tired and too guilty. When Sean had asked her to go to the Bacchanal with him, she *should* have told him no, sorry, I have a boyfriend. Instead she had babbled and evaded until he'd kissed her. She was a thoroughly rotten person. The first thing she would do the next day was see Sean Valletti and blow him off. Great, one more thing to worry about.

Even though she wasn't interested in walking a mile or more through the dark with nothing for accompaniment but a guilty conscience, Summer was not entirely grateful when J.T. pulled over and offered to drive her home. She had the feeling that he would use the opportunity for a talk. And she wasn't sure she was up for it.

"So did they take care of you waitresses?" J.T.

asked as she climbed into his car, a wonderfully decrepit old Dodge Dart.

"A hundred–dollar bill, over and above the fifteen percent," Summer said.

"Hmm. Lianne and Marquez and I only got fifties," J.T. said, giving Summer a dubious look. "Must be they didn't like my legs as much as yours."

Summer shook her head in real annoyance. "I told him not to do that," she said. "See, I know that one guy, the young one, from back home. But I'll split the extra with you guys so that everything's fair."

J.T. laughed. "No, no, keep it. I was just giving you a hard time."

"Yeah, well, Marquez won't take that same attitude," Summer said.

"Marquez," he said, without elaborating.

She waited to see if he would add anything, but all he did was shake his head a couple of times, obviously lost in some internal dialogue.

"You really think Marquez is an artist?" Summer asked.

"You've seen her room, right?"

"But she says that's just a hobby," Summer said.

"Does it look like it's just a hobby? Ever seen her actually working on it?" He smiled fondly. "It's a real sight. I went over there once, banged on her door for about twenty minutes. She wouldn't answer, so I went in, right? Marquez is wearing this dress, a very expensive dress, something you'd wear out to someplace nice. Only, she's past caring about the dress, because it's totally destroyed with paint. She was like . . . like I don't know what. It's probably a bad analogy, but she reminded me of a punker guitar player, just spazzing out, lost to all contact with the regular world. In a frenzy, that's the word. I stood there for twenty minutes watching her, and I swear she never even noticed I was there. After a while I left quietly because I realized she was in a place that was just for her. I don't know. Maybe she let me watch so I would understand something about her. Or maybe she wasn't even able to see me."

Summer thought about this for a moment. At one level it made her terribly jealous. It would be wonderful to be that driven by something . . . anything. "The other day she had paint on her . . . on her body."

"I'm not surprised. Our little rescue mission to find you and Seth probably got her fired up."

"See, it's hard for me to see Marquez as being that way. She's always in such control. Except when she's dancing."

"Marquez thinks she's in control," J.T. said. "She actually believes this junk about living some straight, normal life. Why do you think we broke up?"

"I don't know. All she ever says is that you started getting weird when . . . when you realized you and your parents weren't——"

"Related?" J.T. offered. "Yeah, I know Marquez's

story. She doesn't want to deal with other people's problems. She wants to be around nice, normal, sensible people. Everything cool and ironic and detached."

Summer nodded, understanding suddenly. "She can't be around complicated emotional situations or people who are out of control. She's afraid that she'll lose control."

"Yeah. She's afraid she'll suddenly be what she really is. Because, you see, when she loses that control she becomes this out-there creature who doesn't care about anything but putting an image down on a wall."

They had arrived at their destination, but now Summer felt reluctant to break the contact with J.T.

"Hey, you've never seen my house, have you?" she said lightly.

"The stilt house, right? Only from the water, passing by. When I was a kid we used to think it was inhabited by trolls and orcs." He laughed in embarrassment. "Too much Tolkien, I think."

"I haven't seen any trolls," Summer said. "The occasional cockroach, maybe."

She led him down the pathway that passed the Olan house. She felt vaguely guilty that she hadn't spoken to Diana in a while.

Maybe I'm becoming like Marquez, Summer thought. Maybe I'm avoiding Diana because she's complicated.

They crossed the dark lawn, which sloped gently

down toward the bay. The stilt house came into view as they turned left along the retaining wall. It was a black silhouette against a star-bright sky. Summer wondered if Diver was up top on his deck. She saw nothing, but that didn't prove he wasn't there. When in doubt, Diver's instinct seemed to be to remain invisible.

She gave J.T. the tour of the house, a tour that took all of twenty seconds as she pointed out the obvious—kitchen, bathroom, everything else.

J.T. stopped beside her bed, staring at something.

The framed picture of her family.

He picked it up gently, holding it closer for examination. Summer felt a chill tingle up her spine.

"Are these—" he asked.

"My parents," Summer acknowledged. And maybe yours, she added silently.

J.T. nodded solemnly. "They're a good-looking couple." He turned to face her and held the picture up next to his face. "See any family resemblance?"

He no doubt intended it as a funny question, but it came out wrong. He could not hide the pleading element in his voice.

When Summer said nothing, his self-mocking expression crumbled. Carefully he put the picture back on the nightstand. Then, with one finger, he touched the face of Summer's mother. His brow was furrowed in concentration.

"I don't know these people," he said at last.

"You wouldn't, I guess," Summer said. "You were

just two years old at the time. I mean, if it's true."

"Still," he said. "Two years old . . . shouldn't I remember something? I remember things from when I was little, but it's all disconnected stuff, just images, bits and pieces, like anyone has. Toys. Going to get a shot at the doctor. Laughing really hard when someone was tickling me. This cool little car I had. A pair of pants that were too scratchy. There's nothing there. I don't even have any way of knowing how old I was, and those memories aren't *important* because little kids don't know what's important. I mean, when I was two I don't exactly remember who was president or what was going on in the Middle East. Kids remember dumb stuff. Falling off a swing, that's a big event."

"I'm sorry." It was all Summer could think of to say. "I don't know how we're ever going to figure this out. You and I do look alike, but you look a little like Brad Pitt too, so I don't know."

"Yeah, I've been over and over all this in my mind," J.T. said. "What do we have? I know that I'm not biologically related to my parents. I know that I couldn't find a birth certificate for myself, and I had to use a baptism certificate to get my driver's license. Why? I don't know. Then Marquez tells me that you lost a brother who would be just my age. And she says she's seen us do things or say things at the same time, as if there's some kind of psychic link."

Summer started to say something, then hesitated. What was she going to say? Are you the boy in white who keeps appearing in my dreams? That would sound slightly insane.

"What?" J.T. asked. Then he wiggled his eyebrows. "See? I *knew* you were about to say something. Proof!"

They both laughed, the mood momentarily a little lighter.

"I was just going to ask you . . . do you ever have dreams about the past?"

He shrugged. "I don't have many dreams, I guess. Or at least when I do, I usually forget them within a minute or two of waking up."

"Oh."

"Why do you ask?" He looked at her closely.

"I don't know. They say dreams tell you things sometimes."

"If they do, then they aren't speaking very clearly to me," J.T. said.

"This is going to sound like a strange question," Summer said. "But when you were saying you remembered things from your childhood—you know, like toys and all—was one of them a red ball?"

He smiled. "A red ball? Was that what Jonathan . . . I . . . had when he, or I, disappeared?"

"No one really knows. Forget it," she said.

Silence fell between them, and J.T. returned his gaze to the picture. Summer could see he was trying to find something in it that would open up his dark past. Some explanation.

"I'm going to have to ask them, aren't I?" J.T. said softly.

There was no doubt in Summer's mind whom J.T. meant by *them*. His parents. The people he had always believed were his mother and father.

"The only problem is, do I really want to know the truth?"

Then, surprisingly, his usual devil-may-care smile was back, like the sun poking unexpectedly through storm clouds. He took Summer's hand and met her gaze. "I know one thing. I'd be proud to be your big brother."

Summer looked past him at the picture of her parents. If it was true . . .

Sixteen years of grieving would be ended. A miracle would have occurred.

"I'd be proud to be your little sister too," Summer said.

7

Jonathan Leaves Footprints, and Diana Swings the Pendulum Just a Wee Bit Too Hard.

Summer went to sleep worried that she would be haunted by some nightmare from hell involving not only small boys dressed all in white, but also Seth Warner and Sean Valletti. The idea of all those elements coming together—especially Seth and Sean—was almost enough to keep her awake.

But when she woke she remembered no dreams at all. She did, however, notice a pounding noise like the worst headache on earth. It took several seconds of blank, stupid staring before she realized it actually was pounding and not a headache.

"Who is it?" she yelled, sounding cranky.

"Are you decent?" It was Seth's voice.

"Oh. Seth? Come in!" she yelled. She did not stir from the bed, but pulled the covers higher. She was wearing her usual sleep attire—a baby-tee and boxers. She quickly turned over her pillow after noticing a drool spot. Seth might be grossed out.

The door opened and he came in, looking like a parody of a blue-collar romance hero—tool belt, tight-fitting T-shirt, well-worn and paint-splattered Levi's, clunky brown work boots.

"What, you're still in bed?" he asked incredulously.

"I couldn't get to sleep last night," Summer muttered. Mostly because I was racked with guilt over having let Sean Valletti kiss me.

Seth came over to the bed and sat on the edge of it. He bent down and kissed her lightly on the lips.

"I probably have morning breath," Summer said. "And speaking of morning, why are you here? Not that I'm not glad to see you."

"I told you I was coming to put molding in your bathroom and lay in a line for cable," he said. "All part of the original work order from your aunt."

"She actually said I should have cable TV down here?" Summer asked skeptically.

"Well . . . she said I should fix whatever needed fixing and do whatever needed to be done to make this place livable. And how am I going to hang out with you down here if you don't get ESPN? Don't make me choose between you and the Milwaukee Brewers."

Summer wrapped her arms around his neck and with sudden force pulled him onto the bed beside her. "If you have to choose, I'd better win." She kissed him deeply, with intensity spurred at least in part by the guilty memory of Sean.

"Why, Ms. Smith," Seth protested, "I'm only here to install your cable. What kind of guy do you think I am?"

"I don't know," Summer said in as sultry a voice as she could manage at that hour of the morning. "Are you the kind of guy who would do something really wonderful and exciting for me?"

"Yes, I am," Seth said, not fooled.

Summer collapsed onto his chest and closed her eyes. "Then make me some coffee, because I'm sleepy."

She managed to stumble to the bathroom and subject her body to toothpaste, soap, and deodorant by the time Seth had coffee ready.

She had also managed to run every possible scenario regarding the question of Sean Valletti through her head. They boiled down to two simple options: tell Seth, or don't tell Seth. If she told Seth, he might blow it all out of proportion. If she didn't tell Seth and he later found out, he was certain to blow it all out of proportion.

The unanswered question was, what was the *right* proportion?

"Thanks," she said, accepting a cup from him.

They decided to go outside. They circled the walkway that formed a narrow deck all the way around the stilt house, leaning against the railing and sipping coffee in silence for a while as they watched boat traffic move in and out of the bay. Little boats, big boats, sailboats, Jet Skis, windsurfers. It was a beautiful day, not too horribly humid, with the heat still many hours away from its afternoon peak. The sky was a perfect cornflower blue, with all the clouds gathered neatly together, far off to the east.

Frank the pelican was away from his usual perch, off for a day of dive-bombing fish. Diver was missing from his perch too. Off early, as usual, to a day of doing whatever it was Diver did.

"So what happened to you last night?" Seth asked, yanking Summer away from her contemplation of the sky.

"What do you mean?" Summer demanded in a too-loud voice. She could feel herself blushing.

"I mean, we were going to get together after you finished working that boat party," he said. No sign that he was suspicious.

"Oh, right," Summer said. "Well, it was J.T. After we got done, which was later than we expected, he wanted to talk. You know, about all that stuff."

Seth nodded sympathetically. "How is he doing? How are *you* doing?"

"I think it's harder for him," Summer said. "Much harder. If it turns out to be true, if he is Jonathan, I gain a brother, and my parents find their long-lost son. But J.T. suddenly has to find a new place in the world. He has a new name, a new history, a new family."

Seth whistled sympathetically. "What are you guys going to do?"

"I don't know," Summer admitted. "None of

this has really penetrated. I mean, it all still seems so unreal. I guess I'm just lying back and waiting to see what *he* does. I sure can't tell my parents about it. Not until it's definite."

"How about footprints?"

"Huh? Footprints?"

"Yeah. Most hospitals take a footprint when a baby is born. You know, it's like a fingerprint, except I guess with babies the fingers are too tiny to use. If you know which hospital Jonathan was born at, maybe you can send away for the records."

Summer just stared at him.

"I mean, it would tell you for sure, one way or the other. You would know once and for all whether Jonathan is alive and living right here on Crab Claw Key. Get them to FedEx the stuff and you could have proof within a couple of days."

The first call, the first of what would be many calls, came in at ten-thirty in the morning, just after Diana had finished working out to a TV exercise show. Diana hadn't performed anything like real exercise in at least a year, perhaps more, and she found she was easily exhausted. Long before the half-hour show was over, Diana had grown sullen, spending more and more time coming up with imaginative insults to throw at the insanely perky exer-witch.

Still, she told herself, it was exercise, of a sort. A small step of progress away from lying around in bed most of the day. There were actual beads of sweat on her forehead. That had to count for something.

Her mother appeared in the doorway. She had "home" hair at the moment, which was to say hair of a normal human size, not the bouffant monstrosity she wore out in public because she thought that was what her fans expected of a successful romance novelist.

Mallory looked suspicious. "There's someone on the phone for you," she said, eyeing her daughter closely.

"Uh-huh. So?" Diana wondered if it was one of the agents from the FDLE. She hadn't told her mother about going to the police. Mallory had tried to stop her from pursuing an action against the Merricks. Partly out of justifiable fear of the Merrick millions, partly out of self-interest—the Merrick family owned a piece of Mallory's publisher.

"So he says his name is Mark DeWayne," Mallory said. "Do you know someone named Mark DeWayne?"

That wasn't the name of any of the cops Diana had met. "Never heard of him."

She levered herself up off the floor, where she had been stretching out, and went to the phone in the kitchen. Her mother followed close behind.

"Yes?"

"Is this Diana Olan?" a voice asked.

"Yes, that's me. Who is this?"

He identified himself as Mark DeWayne, a producer for *The Last Word*.

Diana met her mother's anxious gaze. "*The Last Word?*" she said clearly, enjoying the dawning look of dark worry on her mother's face. *The Last Word* was the new challenger to the more established TV tabloid shows such as *Hard Copy* and *Inside Edition.*

"Yes," Diana said in response to the next question, still holding her mother's gaze. "Yes, I *did* level certain charges, as you say. I spoke with the Florida Department of Law Enforcement the day before yesterday."

Mallory's eyes flew open wide. Her lip was trembling with suppressed rage. She seemed poised to rush forward, perhaps hang up the phone.

"And you are the daughter of Mallory Olan, the writer?"

"Yes, my mother is the famous writer," Diana said, enjoying the moment. "You're probably curious about how she's reacting to this too, right?"

Mallory froze.

"Well," Diana said, "of course my mother's been very supportive. What kind of mother would be anything but supportive?" She sent her mother a look of cold triumph. From this moment on, Diana was in charge. What could Mallory possibly do, now that everything was going public? If she failed to support her daughter, she would look like an unfeeling monster.

"I haven't decided whether I want to do any interviews," Diana said. "I mean, the FDLE guys advised me not to talk to people like you, no offense. So I'm going to have to think about it."

She listened a moment longer. One more surprise for Mallory. "Yes, there is a tape," Diana said.

Her mother rocked back, pressing her palm against the counter for support.

"A videotape," Diana said. "Sure, I can confirm that. The FDLE has a copy and I have a copy. What does it show? It shows Ross Merrick confessing, and it shows the senator trying to intimidate me."

To Diana's surprise, her mother did not faint. On the contrary, she laughed, a dry, amused, perhaps amazed sound.

A few minutes later, after repeated and increasingly annoyed refusals to sit for an interview, Diana hung up the phone.

Mallory began clapping her hands, slow, ironic applause. "You're a piece of work, aren't you?" she asked.

"Am I?"

"Oh, yes," Mallory said. "You have one of the richest, most powerful families in America shaking in its boots."

"I guess I do. Plus the other thing."

"Which is?"

"I also have one of the biggest romance writers in the country shaking in *her* boots."

Mallory bit her lip and said nothing. Diana moved close, close enough for her harsh whisper to be heard clearly. "You had your chance to decide who to support, *Mother*."

"I was only trying to protect you," Mallory protested.

Diana laughed derisively. "Sure you were. You were trying to protect me. All you cared about was the well-being of your daughter. And that's the story I'll keep telling everyone . . . which is a good thing, because if I didn't, if I told people you tried to destroy evidence because you wanted to protect your career . . . I guess after that got out, you wouldn't *have* much of a career."

Mallory took a deep, steadying breath. "Diana, whatever you think, I do love you."

"I love me too," Diana said. "Now."

Just then Summer opened the kitchen door and came in. Reading the mood, her face went from sunny to guarded in an instant.

"Is this a bad time?" Summer asked.

"No, not at all," Diana said brightly. "This is a great time."

"Hi, Aunt Mallory," Summer said.

"Summer. Well, I've barely had a chance to see you since you got here," Mallory said. "We'll have to remedy that. But right now I have a little headache."

Summer started to answer, but her aunt was already on her way out of the room.

"Sense a certain tension in the air?" Diana asked gleefully.

"Kind of," Summer answered neutrally. "Were you guys planning World War Three or something?"

Diana laughed, saw that her laughter had startled Summer, and laughed all the harder.

"I, um, just was wondering if you'd seen my video camera," Summer said, looking mightily uncomfortable. "I couldn't find it. I use it to send tapes to my friend."

Diana just laughed harder. "I have a very interesting story to tell you about your video camera," she said. "Come on, we'll get it, and then you and I—and why not, we'll even pick up Marquez—we'll all go shopping or something."

"Are you all right?" Summer asked skeptically.

"I'm the greatest I've ever been," Diana said. "And you know what, Summer? You helped start it all."

"Me? What did I help start?"

"Everything. You know what you said to me the day after the whole big thing at the Merrick estate? You remember, the next day? You told me thanks. For coming to make sure you were okay, and for telling you everything. *Thanks.* That's what started it."

Diana realized she was babbling, but she didn't care. Summer looked as if she was measuring the distance to the nearest exit, but that just made Diana want to laugh again.

"See, you said thanks, and I started thinking, thanks for what?"

"Because you had taken a risk to protect me," Summer said.

"Exactly. You said I was brave. And I thought about it, and after a while I started to wonder if maybe you weren't right. And then I started thinking, you know, Diana, maybe if you were brave for Summer, you could be brave for yourself, because what it all comes down to in the end is that you have absolutely no one in the world but yourself. And from that the whole answer became clear."

"What answer?"

"The answer to why I should live rather than die," Diana said simply.

"So . . ."

"The answer is revenge. Hurt everyone who ever hurt you. Hurt them worse than they hurt you. Hurt them until they never want to hurt you again."

It was obvious, really, now that she understood it.

And yet Summer was looking at her with pain in her eyes. Pain and concern.

"Come on," Diana said, "let's go do something."

"Okay," Summer said reluctantly. "Just remind me not to make you mad."

8

Hairy Chests, Tape, and Doing the Right Thing with Each

*I*t was an unusual get-together, to say the least.

Summer, Diana, and Marquez, sunglassed, sandaled, and bare-midriffed, occupied an outdoor table on the deck of the appropriately named Marina Deck restaurant. They had before them various extravagant, rapidly wilting salads and sweating cold beverages. The sun was high in the sky, but only their bare legs stuck out from beneath the shade of the umbrella.

One of the unusual parts was the conversation, which had started with Diana's incredible tale of the video camera and moved to Summer's even more incredible tale of the underwater cave and her long-lost brother.

The other unusual part was that while Summer was behaving like herself, Diana and Marquez seemed to have switched personalities. Marquez was acting just short of sullen, while Diana, of all people, was the life of their little party, giddy, witty, flirting with the waiter, and admiring the parade of passing men in shorts and trunks and Speedos.

They were down just a little from the Crab 'n' Conch, overlooking the marina. The large boat— Sean Valletti's uncle's boat—was still parked at the far end of the pier.

"Footprints," Diana said, nodding her head sagely. "Sounds like a good idea to send for them. Seth is always very practical that way. The kind of guy who's good with his hands, if you know what I mean, and, Summer, I'm sure you know what I mean." Diana wiggled her eyebrows suggestively.

Summer exchanged a look with Marquez. Yes, Diana was definitely acting strangely.

"You know, Summer, I thought for a while there that I might take a quick pass at Seth myself," Diana chatted away. "I mean, he is cute, isn't he?"

"I think so," Summer said darkly.

"He has a better behind than anything I've seen here on the boardwalk." Diana laughed. "Don't worry, just kidding, Summer. I've decided against that." She took a long sip of her virgin strawberry daiquiri. "But now that I'm back, well, I'm *back*. Just because Adam was a disaster doesn't mean I should become a nun."

"I'm sure the sisters at the convent will breathe a sigh of relief," Marquez muttered. "Do you have a guy in mind? Or will this be someone you call from the fiery pits with a pentagram and a Black Mass?"

"That's better, *Maria*," Diana said patronizingly, patting Marquez's knee. "See, Summer? *Maria's* finally waking up."

Marquez made a halfhearted attempt to stab Diana's hand with a straw.

"Actually, there is a guy—" Diana began.

Summer cut her off with a karate chop in the air. "Shh. Turn around. Don't look!" She turned away from the boardwalk, rested her elbows on the table, and cradled her head in her hands.

"Where? What are we looking at?" Diana demanded, rising from her chair to look around.

"I said, *don't* look!" Summer hissed.

"Oh, I know what she's hiding from," Marquez said, with a glint of her usual mischief. But to Summer's relief, Marquez too shielded her face from view.

"Now, *there* is a specimen," Diana said. "Great shoulders."

"Diana. Will. You. Sit. Down?" Summer said through gritted teeth.

Diana sat down abruptly. But it was too late. Sean had spotted her, and from spotting her, had spotted Summer.

"Summer!" he yelled, plowing through a passing flock of in-line skaters.

"What am I going to say?" Summer asked Marquez. "He's going to ask me out."

Marquez shrugged.

"Pretty sure of yourself, aren't you?" Diana asked grumpily. "What am I? Skank woman?"

"No, you're just schizo," Marquez said. "Look, Summer knows this guy from back in Mootown."

"Hey, Summer, I almost didn't see you," Sean said as he arrived. Instantly he bent over and placed a quick kiss on her cheek. Then he grabbed a vacant chair and pulled it over to the table, sitting between Summer and Diana.

He was wearing trunks and no shirt, still Minnesota pale but reddening. Summer noticed that he had actual chest hair. She had not encountered much chest hair before, and it disturbed her a little. Seth was completely smooth. Boyish. Sean managed to look as if he was ten years older somehow.

"Sean Valletti, this is Marquez, and Diana Olan. Diana is my cousin."

"You're one of the waitresses from last night, right?" Sean asked Marquez. "What kind of a name is Marquez?"

"Japanese," Marquez said.

"Oh, I get it," Sean said after a moment's hesitation. He turned his attention to Diana. "You two are cousins, huh? You don't look at all alike."

"Well, we're not biologically related," Diana explained. "I mean, Summer's father is my mother's brother, but my mother was adopted, so, see, no actual blood relation."

Sean looked doubtful. "Are you pulling my leg? Some kind of a joke, right?"

"No, it's true," Summer said. She was shifting away from him slightly and glancing over her shoulder every few seconds, hoping that Seth was not done with his work, and that if he *was* done, he had not decided to go for a walk by the marina.

"I didn't know that," Marquez said. She made a gesture of relief. "Thank God. I couldn't figure out how good and evil could come from the same family tree like that."

"So, Summer," Sean said, "we on for the Bacchanal?"

"Um . . . ," Summer began.

Marquez and Diana both waited attentively. Sean smiled his toothy smile and unconsciously rippled the muscles of his chest as he leaned close.

"Um, I may have to work that night. I'll have to see," Summer temporized.

Sean surprised her by taking her hand between both of his. "Try hard, okay? I feel like I had to come all the way here to realize what I was missing back home, you know? But now that we're both here, why not?"

"I thought you were seeing Liz Block," Summer said, trying again to find a graceful way to resolve everything without having to tell him no. Actually having to tell Sean Valletti no was not something she had ever expected to do. She wasn't any more prepared for it than she was for blowing off Keanu Reeves.

Sean waved his hand dismissively. "History. I had to end that. I mean, she's sweet and all, but she's not very interesting. To be honest, it was because she was great-looking. You know?" He smiled a dazzling smile. "But you . . . you have the looks and the brains."

"Thanks," Summer said, blushing in a way she hoped was invisible in the shade of the umbrella.

"So make it happen, all right?" Sean said. He got to his feet. "Gotta go now. Nice to meet everyone." He pointed an index finger at Summer. "You and me at the big party."

And then he was gone.

Marquez and Diana both sipped their drinks and said nothing.

"All right, *what?*" Summer demanded angrily.

"I didn't say anything," Diana protested. "Did you say anything, Marquez?"

"Not me."

"Look, what was I supposed to do?" Summer pleaded. "He's *Sean Valletti*. He's the cutest guy in my school. Every girl in school dreams about him. I had a crush on him for years."

"I can see why," Diana admitted. "Great body. Great hair. Great face. I'm undecided on the chest hair."

"I kind of like the chest hair," Marquez said. "I mean, the way he has it—mostly on his chest, not on his stomach or on his shoulders or anything gross."

"He's not exactly a genius," Diana said.

"But that's good, not bad," Marquez said. "You don't want a guy who's too smart. J.T. is too smart for his own good. Always analyzing everything and getting all confused. What you want is a guy who's just good-looking and basically sweet."

"Like Diver," Marquez and Diana said at exactly the same moment.

"I mean, *like* Diver, as one possible example," Diana said quickly, blushing furiously. "Not necessarily Diver himself. He was just the first example that came to mind."

"Uh-huh," Marquez said. She smiled and shook her head. "I'd forget about Mr. Diver. Getting through to the mysterious Mr. Diver is like nailing Jell-O to the wall. Whenever you think maybe something is going on, he's out of there."

"You're probably right," Diana said neutrally.

"Whereas, say, Sean Valletti is right out front, hairy chest and all," Marquez said.

"I'm going to tell him no," Summer said defensively. "I'm *not* going out with Sean. I am totally committed to Seth. I'm going out with him tonight. It's just . . ."

"The end-of-August thing?" Marquez suggested. "Maybe you should think about it. I mean, pretty soon Seth goes one way and you . . . *and* Sean . . . go another way."

"Ah." Diana nodded, understanding. "I get it. Either the summer ends with tearful farewells and broken hearts, or it ends with Summer arriving back home with the coolest guy in her school. Wow."

"Both of you shut up. I'm not even thinking about that," Summer said, annoyed and impatient, as she often was when she was lying.

Diana felt strangely exhausted by the day spent with Summer and Marquez. She had the feeling she might have talked too much, revealed too much of herself, and that kind of thing always gave her the willies. Sometimes, like the song said, she gave herself the creeps.

There was a surprise waiting for her when she got back home. A very large white van was parked just down the street. As she drove past it and pulled into her driveway, two people literally leaped from the back, followed by a third a few seconds later.

By the time she had turned off the ignition and opened the door of her little Neon, a camera was in her face, a light brighter than the sun was in her eyes, and a woman seemed to be trying to force-feed her a microphone.

"Diana! Diana!" the woman shouted. "Are you Diana Olan? I'm Wendy Rackman, *The Last Word.* You are Diana Olan, right?"

Diana squinted into the light and said, "No, I'm Maria Marquez. I'm just a friend of Diana's."

The reporter sagged a little. "Oh. Okay, what do you know about this situation between Diana Olan and Senator Merrick?"

Diana shrugged. "Look, I told your producer on the phone I wasn't sure if I was going to talk to reporters," she said, abandoning the lame pretense.

"So you *are* Diana Olan?" The reporter came alive again.

"Yes. Now would you go away?" Diana turned to go inside.

"Diana, Ross Merrick says you're just an embittered former girlfriend of his brother, Adam, and that you tried to extort money from them with a made-up story about an attempted rape."

Diana stopped with her hand on the doorknob. Obviously the reporter was simply trying to goad her. And just as obviously it had worked.

"If you don't talk to us, Diana, we have to go with Ross's version of events. We'll have no other choice," the reporter said.

Diana shrugged. "There's Ross's version and there's my version, and then there's the videotape. So I guess when the cops release the videotape, the truth will be obvious to everyone."

"Diana, the Merrick family's lawyers say they can keep that videotape out of court, if this case even goes to trial."

"What do you mean?" Diana asked sharply.

"Diana," the reporter said, affecting a sincere tone, "evidence can be suppressed by smart lawyers sometimes. But no one can stop the free press from showing the world the truth. If you give us a copy of the tape, we can have it on the air by tonight. After that, no one will ever be able to suppress the truth."

"I'm *not* going to let you have the tape," Diana said firmly. "I told the police I wouldn't." She had also promised Adam.

Just then the door opened. Mallory came out, hurriedly made up but camera-ready. "Diana, why don't you come inside?"

"Ms. Olan, your daughter's story needs to be told," the reporter said.

"I'll handle this," Diana told her mother, making no attempt to hide her annoyance at the intrusion.

"I think you should talk to me first," Mallory said.

Diana looked uncertainly from the predatory reporter to her mother. "What, you're offering to help me? Why?"

"Excuse us a moment," Mallory told the reporter. She pulled Diana inside and closed the door.

"You don't really understand what you've unleashed, do you?" Mallory asked. "All you're thinking about now is lashing out. You want to hurt the Merricks, fine, but they won't just lie down and play dead."

"What can they do to me?" Diana asked.

"There's an old saying, Diana, something like, 'If you strike at a king, make sure you kill him.' The point being, make sure you don't leave him a chance to hit back."

"Are you telling me I *should* let them see the videotape?" Diana asked, incredulous.

Mallory nodded, her face grim. "It's about who gets to write the story, Diana. The Merricks know how to use the media. They are professionals. Either the Merricks write the story, or *you* write the story. The tape will destroy them."

"I don't get this. Why are you suddenly on my side?"

"I've always been on your side," her mother said wearily. "Whatever you may think about me. I was—I am—afraid of the Merricks. Afraid for me, true, but also for you." She smiled crookedly. "I'm sorry if that isn't pure enough for you. I know a perfect mother would never think of herself at all, but I'm not a perfect mother. I had to think of what this could do to my career. And I also had to think about what all this could mean for you. Wanting to hurt people, even those who hurt you, is a bad thing."

"How else can you keep them from hurting someone else?" Diana demanded.

Her mother shook her head. "I don't know. It's just that when I saw my only daughter about to get into a fight, I wanted to stop it. But now it's too late. It's already begun, so now you have no choice but to try your best to win."

Diana hesitated. "I . . . Adam. You remember when he came to see me? I promised him I wouldn't give the tape to the media."

"Look, it's your choice, Diana," her mother said. She smiled ruefully. "This is a bad time for me to suddenly realize that you're an adult, but this is an adult choice. The tape will hurt them very badly."

Diana considered this for a moment. The image that came to mind was of the pills she had, again and again, counted out into her hand. The pills she had planned to take to end her life.

"I want to hurt them," she said at last.

9

So in any case, Jennifer, now you can see why I
haven't sent you a videotape lately. Like I said,
this whole summer vacation keeps going off in one
unusual direction after another. I thought I'd be
down here all summer and have nothing to tell you
except how my tan was doing. It's good, by the
way. I have achieved major, definite tan lines.

But, see, I figured that would be all I'd have to
tell you about. That, and maybe I'd meet a guy or
something. Instead, I keep meeting additional
guys, which brings me to the one thing I haven't
told you yet. Guess who is down here on Crab
Claw Key? If I gave you a week to guess, you'd
never get it right.

Sean Valletti. Yes, *the* Sean Valletti. He's down
here with his uncle, who has this huge boat. But
the amaze-o thing is that he asked me out.

Yes, Sean Valletti asked me out, and he even kissed me.

I will pause for a moment while you pick yourself back up off the floor, since I bet you fainted.

He wants me to go to this big festival of a dead pirate called the Bacchanal. They say it's like Mardi Gras, kind of. Anyway, Sean actually asked me to go to it with him.

Not that I'm going, of course. I mean, I am totally and completely in love with Seth. Really.

The only reason I didn't tell Sean no right away is because . . . well, he is Sean Valletti, right? Liz Block and Annie Bashears and that Elise girl, all those supposedly popular girls, all those cheerleader creatures, would totally have to *die* if I showed up back in Bloomington with Sean. Summer Smith and Sean Valletti? No one would even believe it if they didn't see it.

It would be like, "Hah, so there!" Like I was magically transported from the level of "Oh, she's not bad, but she's kind of into getting good grades" to "Whoa, she's going with Sean Valletti."

Actually, though, I'm not sure I like Sean that much. He's cute, but that's about all he is. So even if we broke up after we got back to Bloomington, it would be okay.

Seth is a whole different story, Jen. I mean, Seth makes me sick. No, wait, that came out wrong. What I meant was, sometimes I'm lying in bed at night and I can't go right to sleep and I start thinking about Seth . . . and I just really wish he were there. I mean, in this powerful way. Like if I think about him ever breaking up with me, I get a sick feeling.

That's what I meant by making me sick. I feel that way right now, talking to you about it, even thinking about it. Kind of like really bad cramps combined with running too much in gym.

Marquez . . . I've told you how Marquez isn't exactly subtle . . . anyway, she keeps reminding me about the end of summer, when I have to go home. What am I supposed to do then? Seth and I are going to be at the airport, right where we met and where he first kissed me, and I'm going to get on one plane, and he's going to get on another, and it's going to be the worst day of my life.

See? I'm starting to get all weepy just thinking about it.

I should have just stayed home for the summer. I would have been miserable, but not *that* miserable. Not to be all psychological or anything, but maybe that's why I haven't told Sean to go away. I mean, maybe part of me *wants* to keep Seth at arm's length. It's just so totally superficial with Sean it's almost a relief. . . . I don't know. It's stupid. Because in the end I'm in love with Seth, and summer's almost over, and I am going to be totally destroyed.

Still, the thing I keep thinking is, how can I really be sure what's going to happen in the future? I mean, did I think I was suddenly going to run into Jonathan? A guy who might be my own brother reappears from nowhere. That's practically a miracle. So who knows, right? Who knows what could happen by the end of summer? Maybe it will be something I haven't even thought about.

10

A Little Night Music

Toward the end of the shift, when the orders from the waiters had slowed to a trickle and the cleaning up of the kitchen had begun, J.T. picked a CD and slipped it into the boom box the cooks kept on top of a reach-in refrigerator.

He cranked the volume to seven and hit Play. Offspring doing "Bad Habit." It was one of the kitchen staff's standards. They favored seriously hard-edged rock at the end of a tough night. The worse the night, the wilder the music.

Skeet, one of the other cooks, heard the opening bars and gave J.T. a wink. "It wasn't *that* bad a night," she said.

"Oh, Skeet, you think every night is a Melissa Etheridge night," J.T. teased. He waltzed over, took Skeet by the waist, and drew her into a completely incongruous dance, as if they were keeping time to a different piece of music. "First time you've danced with a guy, Skeet?"

"No, only I prefer guys with some idea of rhythm," Skeet said.

J.T. released her, laughing. "Come on, Tom," he said, inviting the fry cook to dance. "Let's go."

"Yeah, when pigs fly," Tom said.

"No one wants to dance," J.T. complained. Then he spotted Lianne coming through the swinging doors. "Lianne! Dance with me." He snapped his fingers. "I got dancin' feet."

"Dance to this?" Lianne said, turning up her nose.

"Skeet! Stick in Janet," J.T. ordered. Seconds later Janet Jackson came on. But still Lianne refused.

"J.T., we're at work," she said. She gave him a peck on the cheek and went back to the dining room just as Marquez passed through the door.

J.T. retreated a bit, stepping back behind the line and pretending to go back to work. Marquez started to do side work, dipping tartar sauce into little plastic cups, but J.T. knew her too well to think she could ignore the music. Within seconds he could see the effect—a motion beginning with her head, swaying just slightly at first, translated down her neck to her shoulders, her bottom, her legs, topped off by a little twirl with the tartar sauce spoon still in her hand.

J.T. smiled ruefully. The future Harvard girl. The future corporate lawyer.

There wasn't anything wrong in dancing with his former girlfriend, was there? After all, a moment earlier he'd been dancing with Skeet. He'd even asked Tom, although the fry cook was unlikely to be seen as a threat by Lianne. No, he should stick to his work.

Marquez was now dancing far more than she was filling cups of tartar sauce.

J.T. whipped off his apron. Screw it. He had dancin' feet. What was he supposed to do?

He took the spoon from Marquez and set it down.

"Crank it, Skeet," he said.

By the time Lianne reappeared in the kitchen, Marquez was up on the stainless steel counter, hands in the air over her head, hips thrusting, hair loose and flying, doing death-defying moves like some MTV Grind dancer disguised as a waitress. J.T. was dancing more sedately below her, choosing to keep his feet on the ground.

"Is this really—" Lianne began, but the music drowned her out.

She caught J.T.'s eye. He gave her a wan grin and tried to draw her into the moment. But Lianne just looked angry and hurt.

Skeet, sensing the mood, turned the music down. Marquez opened her eyes, annoyed. "What are you— Oh," she said, spotting Lianne. She hopped down from the counter, flushed and perspiring. "Why, Lianne. Thank goodness you got here in time. We were all in danger of having fun."

"Well, that's so *you*, isn't it?" Lianne said. "Always there for the fun, and out the door anytime things get serious."

"Oh, shut up, Lianne," Marquez said dismissively.

"Hey, that's not called for, Marquez," J.T. said, quietly but firmly.

"What? You're defending little Miss Mood-killer?" Marquez demanded.

J.T. told himself just to let it go. Marquez could be volatile when embarrassed, and she had quite a mean tongue when she was mad. But by the same token, he couldn't stand by and let her dump on Lianne.

"Marquez, look, we had some fun, let's not start something," J.T. said.

"I'm not starting anything," Marquez fired back. "It's this life-size Barbie here—"

"Come on, Marquez," J.T. began.

Lianne put a hand on his arm. "Let her say whatever she wants," she said, looking at Marquez with contempt. "It's all she can do—flirt and party and be a witch. It doesn't bother me. I feel sorry for her. She has to put on a big show for everyone to distract them from the fact that she's a cold, selfish person with nothing inside."

"You know nothing about me, Lianne," Marquez said scornfully.

"I know one thing. J.T. is with *me* now because you couldn't be bothered to be there for him."

"I think everyone has said enough," J.T. said.

"Everyone but you, J.T.," Lianne said, suddenly turning on him.

He realized with a shock that there were tears in her eyes. It had never occurred to him that Lianne *could* cry. A quiver had appeared in her voice. "You haven't said the thing you need to say, J.T. You need to tell Marquez it's over, for good, forever. You need to give her up."

J.T. felt stunned. The entire room was quiet. Even the dishwasher was between cycles. "Marquez knows I'm with you, Lianne," he said.

"Yeah. That's why I come in and find you dancing with her," Lianne sneered. "And when you see me you get this little-bad-boy look on your face, like I'm the teacher who caught you throwing spit wads."

"That's not it at all," J.T. protested.

"Then tell her it's over, J.T., because she knows she still has a hold on you," Lianne said sadly. "Marquez isn't stupid. But neither am I."

"I think it's pretty clear, given everything," J.T. tried again.

"I'm out of here," Lianne said suddenly. She bit her lip. "I'll get someone to do my side work for me. I'll be at home, J.T. I guess you'll either come over or you won't."

"Oh, I don't even believe that," Seth said, disgusted. "That's pathetic. They call him out? That was out? He was so safe." He pointed the remote control and clicked off the TV.

"We lost, right?" Summer said, playing dumb. Seth was sitting on her bed. Summer was lying back, her head in his lap.

"Only by three runs," Seth said glumly.

"And we care deeply about this because . . ."

"Because Milwaukee is my team," Seth said.

"But you live in Eau Claire, and isn't Eau Claire actually closer to Minneapolis than Milwaukee?"

"Yes," he agreed patiently. "But that's in Minnesota, not Wisconsin. Besides, the Brewers are so pathetic they need every fan they can get. The Twins have plenty of fans. They don't need me the way the Brewers do. Especially this season, because they really, truly suck."

"Isn't there anything I can do to make you feel better?" Summer said, wiggling her eyebrows suggestively.

"Hmm, I don't know. You don't happen to know any great unemployed pitchers, do you?"

"Fine, you had your chance." She started to get up, but Seth caught her arm and pulled her back.

He put his arms around her, drawing her close, then closer, till her lips touched his. As always, his kisses started sweet and gentle. But each new contact was more intense, more urgent, until soon she was gasping for air, feeling that she wanted to devour him, to go beyond anything their lips could accomplish, to enter his soul and make one person out of two.

She withdrew, holding him away with a hand pressed against his mouth. Her breath was shuddery, her face burning hot. Her mind was a confusion of thoughts and images—none of which her mother would have approved of.

"I wish I had a couch," she muttered.

"What's wrong with the bed?" Seth said in a low voice.

"It's a *bed*, that's what's wrong with it," Summer said.

"You know I'd never ask you to do anything you don't want to do," he said, even sounding sincere. "It doesn't matter if it's a couch or a bed. All you have to do is say no."

She buried her face in the hollow of his neck. "I know. That's not the problem. Saying no is the problem."

He lifted her head and kissed her again. His hand touched her chin, her throat. He moved it down a little farther and—

"No!" Summer said, pushing him away.

"Now, see? That wasn't so hard," he said, grinning. "You say no just fine. Unfortunately."

"It's so easy for guys," Summer complained. "With you it's like an on-off switch. You go till someone stops you, but it always ends up being the girl's decision. We're always the ones who have to have self-control."

"That's not true," Seth protested. "I have to have self-control too. I mean, I wanted to start making out with you an hour ago, but no, I knew I wanted to see the game, so I controlled myself until it was over."

Summer smiled at him affectionately. Then she hit him over the head with a pillow.

She got up and went to her tiny kitchen. On the way she turned on her radio. A raunchy, bluesy Bonnie Raitt song came on. "You want something to eat?" she called over her shoulder.

"What do you have?"

"Um . . ." She opened her refrigerator. "Milk, yogurt, and wilted lettuce." She checked her cupboard. "Cheerios. Instant grits. Sorry—I figured that since this is technically the South, I should try grits. Ah-hah! Pop-Tarts."

"Pop-Tarts! All right," he said enthusiastically. He came to join her as she loaded the toaster. "Life. It just doesn't get any better than this. You and Pop-Tarts."

"While they last," Summer said. Instantly she regretted it, but the thought had popped into her head and straight out through her mouth.

"What do you mean?" he asked. "We're low on Pop-Tarts?"

"Nothing," she said. But suddenly she felt terribly sad. Probably just the result of coming down off the intense high of making out.

But Seth wasn't going to let it go. "Summer, what's the matter?"

"I really . . . really like this. Being with you. Being here. Being here with you," she said. Tears were filling her eyes, and that annoyed her because she was ruining a perfectly good night.

The Pop-Tarts popped up from the toaster, but

before she could grab them, Seth turned her around to face him. "Summer, talk to me. Look at you, you're crying."

"No, I'm not," she said, wiping at her tears. "It's just . . . the end of the summer."

"What about the end of the summer?"

"It's going to come soon, isn't it? Then no more—" She swept her hand around the room. "No more any of this. I'll be in school. In Bloomington. You'll be in school in Eau Claire. I don't even have a car," she said.

"What does a car—"

"In case we ever wanted to see each other, duh. Or did you not even think about that? Are you just assuming we'll never ever be able to see each other again, because I—" She began sobbing, and her words were swallowed up.

"What are you talking about?" he said. "Why are you worrying about the end of August? We have four weeks till then."

"So I shouldn't worry about what will happen because it's a long way off?" she demanded, having brought her vocal cords under some control.

"We could . . . I don't know, we could die tomorrow," he said, looking beleaguered. "I could get crushed by a meteor or something. You could get run over by a bus."

"A meteor?"

"Jeez, Summer, I'm just saying we've barely gotten together, so don't start trying to figure out the whole future." He was compulsively running his hand through his hair and shrugging, both of which were things he did when he was confused.

It wasn't the answer she had been looking for. He sounded almost indifferent. No, that wasn't fair—not indifferent, just puzzled, as if the problem had never occurred to him. He looked as if he'd just been asked to define the entire nature of the universe.

Summer took the Pop-Tarts out of the toaster and handed one to him. "Careful, they're a little hot."

"Summer, you know I love you," he said.

"I love you too," she said in a voice choked by surging tears.

"So everything will work out." He took a bite of his pastry.

But at that moment Summer had the clearest mental image, almost a vision—Seth kissing her one last time in the airport, with tears and promises to get together every chance they had. Slowly he would walk away. He would pause at the gate, turn, and mouth the words *I love you,* and she would mouth the same words back.

And the terrible thing would be that they would both mean them.

Marquez told herself at least a million times that she didn't care. That the last thing she wanted was for J.T. to show up. He was with Lianne, and that was fine with her. He was trouble. Nothing but trouble and heartbreak.

He didn't even respect her. Trying to tell her how she should live her life. Trying to tell her what she was and what she wasn't.

Basically, he was a jerk. Basically, he could drop dead. Basically, he could disappear without a trace and she wouldn't care, because there was absolutely no way that he could ever, conceivably, by the strangest fate she could imagine, ever, ever fit into the life she saw for herself.

Although she hated to think that Lianne was with him at that moment. Not that it was about Marquez wanting *him*. That wasn't it. She just didn't want Lianne to have the satisfaction. Calling Marquez a cold, selfish person with nothing inside—for that, Lianne deserved to be lying alone in her room thinking J.T. really had dumped her to be with Marquez.

Hah. That would show her.

Marquez fell asleep after a while, listening to a Mazzy Star CD—haunting, wispy songs that were like some halfway station between waking and sleep.

She woke suddenly, eyes wide, with the realization that someone had just come into her room. "Who's there?" she demanded of the darkness.

"Me," he said.

She relaxed, sagging back against her pillows. "How did you get in?"

"Key. I remembered where you guys keep the esstra key."

"I'll have to remember to hide it somewhere new."

121

His speech was slurred. Not extremely, but noticeably. He had been drinking. Marquez heard him fumbling around in the dark. Probably looking for the light switch.

"Don't turn on the lights, I'm in bed," she said.

"'Fraid I'll see your jammies?"

"I don't wear jammies," she said coolly. She felt around in the pile of clothes near her bed for an oversize T-shirt and pulled it over her head. "J.T., why are you here?" She could barely make out the hint of his shape, still beside the door, probably leaning against the wall. Half ready to topple over and pass out. Wonderful.

"I wanted to see it," he answered.

"See what?"

"The place where you painted out my name, erased me," he said. "You tole me it was erased."

"J.T., just go away," Marquez said, alarmed now. She *had* told him she'd taken his name off the wall. Unfortunately she had, for reasons that escaped her now, painted him in again. If he saw that, he would get the wrong idea.

Suddenly the overhead lights snapped on. Marquez snatched at her sheets. J.T. was definitely drunk. He was swaying like a tree in a gale. He had on shorts and a T-shirt and, for some reason, a gray raincoat. His hair was a mess. He blinked like a mole in the light, shading his eyes with his hand.

"Jeez, that's bright," he said.

"It just seems that way because your pupils are probably twice their normal size," Marquez said.

122

"I've been drinking. Beer. Also, I've been doing sad things. So don't be all cranky with me, Marquez," he said.

He pried himself away from the wall and walked to the middle of the room. For a long time he just stared. Stared and swayed. He swayed far enough that Marquez leaped out of bed to grab his arm and keep him from falling over.

"You said you painted over me," he said.

"I did," Marquez said. "But it was just this big, empty hole, so I had to put your name back in. Temporarily. Until I can think of something else."

J.T. snorted. "You're such a liar. You lie about everything. You lie about that." He pointed to his name on the wall, huge, 3-D letters that made it the single biggest feature of the mural, bigger by far than it had originally been. "Plus, you lie about . . . everything."

Marquez was tempted to let him go and watch him fall on his face. Instead she walked him over to the bed, lined him up, and with no unnecessary gentleness, pushed him straight back. He fell spread-eagled, faceup.

"I broke up with Lianne," he said to the ceiling.

"Why did you do that?" Marquez demanded. There was a small refrigerator under the Formica and chrome counter. She retrieved a Coke and popped the top.

"She cried," J.T. said, ignoring Marquez's question. "Also cursed."

"Well, you probably shouldn't have broken up

with her," Marquez said, feeling guilty and vaguely triumphant, and then feeling guilty that she felt triumphant.

"Had to," J.T. said. "She wanned to know if I was over you. Guess what the answer was?"

"Drink some of this," Marquez said, sitting beside him and pressing the Coke into his hand. "A little caffeine. Sorry, I don't have a coffee machine here."

He sat up partway and took a long swig.

"I'm messed up," he said sadly. "I don't know what to do anymore. One minute all happy. The next . . . messed up."

Marquez could not think of anything to say.

"I . . . I mean, I don't even know *who* I am anymore. J.T.? Jonathan? I don't know."

"You're whoever you always were," Marquez said impatiently. "But you know, maybe you should see a shrink or something. Get some help."

He nodded and smiled to himself over some secret joke. "Yeah, I need help. I need help. I need someone."

"J.T., look, you know I'm not good at—"

"Not *you*," J.T. sneered. "I don't need you."

"Then what the—"

"Her," J.T. said. He swept the room with his hand, then pointed at the painted walls. "Her, that's who I need. I need the girl who painted all this. Not you."

Marquez swallowed hard. Typical J.T. He just *had* to make everything complicated when it could be so simple. He just *had* to pick at everything.

"Look, J.T., once and for all, I'm me, that's me too, but I have a right to be whatever I choose. I'm not going to be some loser artsy-fartsy type selling crappy paintings to tourists on the boardwalk. So get off it."

But he was looking at the wall, smiling and nodding, ignoring her. "That girl, she's the one I love. She's the one I can't forget. I saw her once, dressed in this gown, this fancy dress, painting and . . . just gone, just not even part of the world anymore. Did you know that?" He focused his bleary gaze on her. His breath reeked of beer. "Did you know I was there and saw you that one time?"

"No," Marquez lied. Why *had* she let him watch her?

To her amazement, since she would not have thought he could walk, he got up and went to the door. But he didn't leave. He switched off the light. "There. Now I don't have to see *her*. I better go."

"J.T., you're too drunk to make it home. You'll fall in front of a truck and get run over."

"I'll bounce right off," he said, giggling incongruously.

Marquez grabbed him rudely by the lapels of his raincoat and marched him back to the bed. She pulled the coat off and pushed him onto the bed.

Under the cover of darkness she unwrapped her sheet partway and spread it over both of them.

For a while she thought he might just have fallen asleep. But then he rolled closer and laid his arm across her stomach. And then, quite naturally, he kissed her.

It was not a great kiss. He was sloppy and smelly.

"I love you," he said.

"Sleep it off," she said roughly. "You'll feel better in the morning."

He held her. "I feel better now," he said.

"J.T., let me just make this clear. I'm not going to make love to you," she whispered.

"I don't need you to *make* love," he said. "Just love me."

Marquez sighed. "Like I have a choice," she said. "Jerk."

He buried his face in her soft explosion of curls and whispered in her ear, "You're not so tough. Just say it."

"J.T., just go to sleep. You're drunk, and you're getting on my nerves," Marquez said irascibly. She closed her eyes. "Okay. So I love you. Big deal. You make one wrong move, and I break your arm."

11

Summer Lies to Herself, While Dolphins Tell the Truth.

The woman on TV was telling Ricki Lake a complicated story having to do with marrying her husband's best friend while she was still married to her husband. But it was okay, she said, because she'd only done it to get close to the live-in girlfriend of the second husband, because they shared an interest in alien abductions. Both of them had at one time been abducted love slaves of the Venusians, who, according to the woman, were really pretty nice people, once you got past the extra eye.

Summer was ironing her work uniform, messing up the annoying pleats because she was paying too much attention to the show. There were footsteps on the deck outside, and Summer found herself hoping it wasn't Seth. Her hair was half done, she was wearing a ratty robe over a ratty T-shirt (having fallen behind on laundry), and besides, she wanted to learn more about the Venusians.

"Who is it?"

"Diana."

"Diana?" Summer said under her breath. "Come in!" she yelled.

Diana was elegant, as always, dressed in a sarong skirt that seemed to be wrapped over a one-piece bathing suit. The striking thing, though, was the big blond wig. She looked like a cool *Glamour* model wearing Dolly Parton's hair.

"Can I come in?" she asked.

"Sure. What's up?" Summer asked, looking pointedly at the hair.

"What do you mean, what's up? Don't you watch TV?" Diana asked.

"We watched baseball last night."

"Too bad. Should have watched *The Last Word*. Suddenly I'm famous, or infamous, or something." She took off the wig and looked at it with amusement. "Nice, huh? It's Mallory's. There are six TV trucks parked out in the driveway. I thought they might spot me coming down here." She tossed the wig on Summer's bed.

"Yeah, I noticed something going on out there. They must have run that tape you gave them, huh?" Summer said.

"Good guess," Diana said dryly. "Now it's like a weasel convention in our driveway, and I have someplace I have to go—without them following me."

"You think they'd actually follow you?"

"Mallory says I should count on it. I'm refusing to say anything more to anyone. She says that otherwise it will look as if I'm trying to exploit the situation." Diana rolled her eyes expressively. "It turns out Mallory is pretty smart about this kind of stuff. I should have known."

"Jeez, Diana," Summer said, "isn't this kind of weirding you out?"

Diana shrugged. "A little, I guess. But it's been a weird year for me. It is gross, yes. Like now the entire country knows who I am, and that Ross tried to rape me. They disguised my face, you know, with one of those fuzzy spots, but that just increases the desire of these other creeps to get a picture."

Summer felt a little overwhelmed. She pulled back her curtain and looked in the direction of the house. Of course, all she could see were the trees that always blocked the land view. Diana seemed cool and in control, but then, Diana had seemed perfectly cool and in control at a time when, Summer now knew, she was actively planning to commit suicide. Cool and in control didn't necessarily mean anything.

"Jeez, Diana," Summer said again, having thought of nothing better to say. This was a situation completely outside her experience.

Diana began unwrapping her skirt. "Anyway, look, I've got places to go, people to see. I want to use one of the Jet Skis under the house."

"Well, they are yours," Summer pointed out.

"As a matter of fact, I was going to say you'd better come with me. That is, if you're going into work. Those guys will jump any warm body that appears, and you'd have to walk right through them. I mean, unless you want to get famous too."

"No," Summer said quickly, alarmed by the idea. She hadn't told her parents about her own near run-in with Ross Merrick. It was just the first of an ever-expanding list of things she hadn't told her parents in their weekly phone calls. She could only hope they hadn't somehow accidentally watched any of the tabloid shows the night before.

"The last time I rode that stupid Jet Ski I was with Marquez, and we ran out of gas," Summer said.

"Come on," Diana said, ignoring her protest. "If you're coming with me, I've got to go." She checked her watch. "I'm going to go to the marina and borrow a car."

Summer began folding her uniform neatly. She wrapped it in a plastic trash bag. "What is this place you have to go to?"

"None of your business," Diana said, softening the harsh statement with a reluctant smile.

They descended through the trapdoor in the floor, and minutes later were skimming across the choppy little waves at what seemed like a hundred miles an hour. It was only her second time, but Summer felt like an old pro on the machine now, flexing her knees to absorb each new shock as the Jet Ski went airborne and crashed, sending up a white plume of warm salty spray. It meant arriving at work wearing a bathing suit, with her hair tangled and salty, but that was nothing very unusual at the Crab 'n' Conch.

And there was such sheer pleasure in flying along under the bright yellow sun, her legs stinging from the force of the water, hot wind whipping her hair, that she wondered why she didn't get to work this way every day.

Diana rode just ahead, her own hair a dark tornado, pushing the speed ever upward, past the point where Summer cared to keep up.

They arrived too soon at the marina, both slowing to meld with the busy to-ing and fro-ing of other craft: white-winged sailboats, colorful windsurfers, and needle-sharp cigarette boats.

Summer glanced over at Mr. Holland's boat. Sean was not on deck, and she felt vaguely relieved. Diana had disappeared, going her own way in the small maze of floating docks.

Summer parked just below the Crab 'n' Conch, tying up the little Jet Ski with what she hoped was professional-looking confidence.

She climbed the ladder, carrying her bag, and went in the back door of the restaurant, where she was promptly informed that she was not on the schedule to work that day. She protested that she was, but a check of the schedule showed that she was not.

Back outside, feeling a little lost since Marquez *did* have to work and Summer had no plans for the day, she felt a shadow fall over her, blocking the sun.

"Hi," Sean said. "Going in to work?"

"Yes," Summer said quickly. She was proud of herself. She was blowing him off. She was blowing off Sean Valletti.

"Cool, then you can wait on me," he said.

"Well, actually . . . ," she said, shifting gears, trying again to get rid of him, "I *was* going into work, but I got my schedule screwed up."

"Better yet." He grinned. "In fact, perfect. I have one of my uncle's cars and I was thinking of driving down to Key West, maybe shop for something for my mom. Her birthday's coming up, and it would be cool to have a girl's advice on what to get."

"I guess I could do that," Summer said.

It sounded perfectly innocent, and she *had* tried twice to get rid of him. She was just going to help Sean shop for a present for his mom. No one could possibly imply that it meant anything. Some article of clothing, Summer thought, yes, that would be best. That way Mrs. Valletti would wear it when she went to PTA stuff, and Summer would be able to point it out to everyone as the thing she had helped Sean pick out when they were in Florida together.

Oh, come on, Summer, she told herself, angrily trying to suppress the guilt, it's just a harmless little way to annoy whichever girl will probably be going with Sean by then, because you certainly won't be.

Harmless. As in no problem. As in no big deal.

Unless they ran into Seth.

*   *   *

132

Diana tied her Jet Ski up in a far corner of the marina. She unpacked her skirt, watch, and purse from the little compartment under the seat, wrapped the skirt around her waist, and jumped two feet straight up when someone said, "Diana!"

But then she recognized the voice, and a wave of pleasure, a very unfamiliar feeling for her, swept over her. Diver. He was standing on the deck of a sailboat a few feet away, wearing his inevitable bathing suit. He jumped down to the dock, causing it to rock sluggishly back and forth.

"Hi, Diver," she said, feeling a little shy.

"Hi, Diana," he said, looking almost as uncomfortable as she felt.

She hadn't seen him since the amazing moment they'd shared on her balcony. He had not grown less attractive. His eyes were no less deep. His lips were still . . .

"Did you come to see me?" he asked.

"To tell you the truth, no," she admitted. "I, um, I wasn't sure if I was ready for that yet. The last time—" She lowered her eyes and stared at the boards, and, incidentally, at his legs. "I wasn't sure if you wanted to see me," she said.

"I thought about it," he said solemnly.

Diana couldn't help but smile. There was something irresistibly sweet about his sincerity. "And what did you decide, Diver?"

"I decided yes."

Diana nodded, satisfied. "Hey, I guess you wouldn't want to go with me, would you?"

"I wouldn't?" He seemed confused.

"What I meant was, maybe you're busy."

"No. I'm not."

"Okay. Then how do you feel about little kids? And dolphins?"

She picked up the car she'd arranged to borrow and drove calmly past yet another TV truck that seemed to be heading out toward the Merrick estate. She sped along the highway, island hopping, feeling wonderfully free at being off Crab Claw Key, and nervous and excited, and incredulous that Diver was sitting beside her.

On the way she told him a little about the Dolphin Interactive Therapy Institute. It used dolphins as a kind of therapy, bringing emotionally damaged children together with the supremely gentle animals. Diana had volunteered there for almost a year.

Diana checked in with her supervisor and introduced Diver to the mostly female staff and volunteers, who, Diana noticed, had the usual response to Diver—overly long handshakes and sappy smiles.

When the introductions were over, Diana went to get her most special charge. "Diver, this is Lanessa," she said as they walked out to the dolphin pool. It was a huge crystal blue tank filled by the waters of the Gulf. There was a covered area, an awning that stretched out over the last few feet of the tank, but beyond it the sun beat down, and the very faint breeze did little to cool the air. "Lanessa, this is my friend Diver."

Diana had expected something like instantaneous rapport between the little girl and Diver. But the first contact was disappointing.

"Hi," Diver said.

Lanessa just looked up at him and sidled behind Diana.

Just then Jerry, Lanessa's favorite dolphin, burst from the water in a high, flying jump with a midair turn.

"He learned that himself," Diana said apologetically. "We don't train them to do any dumb Sea World tricks."

"You wouldn't have to train Jerry," Diver said.

"No, he's always—" Diana stopped. Had she told Diver the dolphin's name? She couldn't remember telling him. But obviously she must have.

Jerry swam to them under the water, surfaced, and began chattering away, bobbing his head at Lanessa as he usually did. Lanessa smiled at the dolphin, as she had for the past couple of weeks. It had taken her more than a month to learn that smile.

"Shall we go in and swim with Jerry today?" Diana asked Lanessa. Sometimes the answer was yes, and then they would stay in the water for a few minutes while Jerry waited patiently for Lanessa to pat his head. Other times, for reasons Diana could not decipher, the answer was no, and they merely watched Jerry.

Today Lanessa just shook her head.

"I don't understand why," Diana said to Diver.

Then, to the little girl, "Should we just watch Jerry play today?"

Lanessa nodded.

It had been a mistake bringing Diver, Diana realized. His presence had upset the equilibrium, had made Lanessa withdraw again. Given her history, she had never been comfortable with any of the male staff or volunteers. Diver was male.

But then Diver leaned over to the little girl. He seemed to be whispering in her ear.

Lanessa nodded. She turned and looked straight at Diana. There was something in that look that sent chills up Diana's spine.

Lanessa pointed at Jerry and tugged weakly at Diana's hand.

"You *do* want to go in?" Diana asked.

"Yes," Lanessa said.

"Should Diver come with us, do you think?"

Lanessa exhibited one of her rare smiles. "Yes."

For an hour they played in the warm water—more real play than Lanessa had ever managed before. She even went for a brief ride on Jerry's back, with Diver holding on to her.

By the time their hour was up, half the staff of the institute was standing by the edge of the pool, watching. They had all seen breakthroughs with the children, but no one had expected to see so rapid a change in Lanessa. Either that, Diana thought, just a bit annoyed, or they were ogling Diver.

She was still a little annoyed on the drive back to Crab Claw Key. On the one hand, she'd had the feeling Diver might make some special contact with the little girl. In a lot of ways Diver was just a big child himself. On the other hand, she hadn't expected it to work as well as it had. On the way out, everyone had made a point of suggesting she bring Diver with her next time she came. It was enough to make her feel a little inferior.

"Jerry is amazing with Lanessa," she said to Diver. "It's too bad, really. He's due to be released in a couple of weeks. We don't want to keep the dolphins prisoner, so we let them go after a while."

Diver nodded. "Yeah, but he doesn't want to go yet. He wants to make sure Lanessa is okay."

Oka-a-a-a-y, Diana thought, glancing at Diver to see if he was joking. "What makes you think he wants to stay on?"

Diver shrugged. Then he smiled ruefully. "I don't want you to think I'm crazy. Summer's not totally sure I'm not crazy, and that Marquez girl, she *is* sure. That I'm crazy."

"I won't think you're crazy," Diana said.

"Well . . . Jerry told me."

Deep breath. "Jerry *told* you?"

"Yes, he wants to make sure Lanessa is okay, but then he does have to go. He has things he wants to do."

"What does he want to do?" Diana asked, curiosity getting the better of her.

Diver looked at her solemnly. "He wants to mate. You know, if he can meet the right female."

Diana giggled, then stopped herself. "Sometimes

I can't always tell when you're kidding," she said.

Diver just looked at her. If he was kidding, he was keeping a very straight face.

"Just out of curiosity," Diana said, "what did you tell Lanessa that got her into the pool?"

Now Diver looked uncomfortable. He stared out of the window, seemingly absorbed by the sight of a beautiful gold and blue windsurfer scooting beneath the causeway.

"What is it, a secret?" Diana asked. "One minute she didn't want to play, the next minute she did. It would be nice to know what you told her. Did you tell her not to be afraid of Jerry? What?"

"She's not afraid of Jerry," Diver said. "She was afraid of you."

Diana stared, dumbstruck. Then she was angry. "Afraid of *me?* What do you mean? She loves me."

"She does. But sometimes you scare her. She can tell when you're angry, even deep down. I don't know what happened to her," he said grimly, "but she knows all about anger. She can feel it, like knowing when a storm is coming. She learned to sense it."

"I am not angry," Diana said angrily. "At least, I wasn't then."

Diver shrugged. "I guess she thought you were. Deep down, maybe. I don't know."

"Yeah, right," Diana snapped. "So what did you tell her? What did you whisper in her ear?"

"I told her not to be afraid, because you were hurt too, just like her."

Diana felt her stomach lurch. Tears sprang to her

eyes, blurring her vision. That was the look Lanessa had given her. Pity. Shared sadness.

"Oh, God," Diana said, brushing furiously at her tears. "Don't ever . . . That's not right. I don't deserve . . ." She took a deep, steadying breath. "Diver, I've read that girl's file. Whatever I've gone through is nothing. It's nothing. Not compared to her. Besides, look, I've hit back. I've gotten revenge, and that has . . . has cured me, made me strong again."

They had arrived back on the key. Diana pulled the car to a stop in the marina parking lot.

"Lanessa can't get revenge," Diver said. "So how will she get strong again?"

"I don't know," Diana admitted. Then she put her hand on Diver's arm. She and Lanessa weren't the only ones with secrets. "Did you, Diver? Did you ever get revenge?"

"No," he said simply.

He got out of the car, but then leaned down to look in the window. "By the way, Jerry says you're the most beautiful human female he's ever seen. He thinks it doesn't matter if you disturb my *wa*. He says it's worth it."

"*Jerry* said that?"

Diver smiled. "Okay, maybe I made up that part."

12

When Fantasies and Enemies Die

Summer's day with Sean Valletti turned out not to be entirely innocent.

They drove to Key West, listening to loud music on the way. This was the most innocent part of the day, since conversation was pretty much impossible as long as Sean had the stereo cranked.

But when they reached Key West and got out to wander the streets in a search for the perfect birthday gift for Mrs. Valletti, conversation became almost unavoidable.

"What kind of things does she like?" Summer asked. She had stashed her uniform back on the Jet Ski and had borrowed a T-shirt from Sean to go over her bathing suit. It turned out to be one of his football jerseys. She was walking around with *Valletti* on her back, above the number twenty-two.

"She likes the usual kind of stuff, I guess," he answered, sounding puzzled by the question. "You know, mom stuff."

"Does she have any hobbies or anything? Does she like to cook? Does she garden? Does she read books?"

He shrugged. "How about some kind of clothing?"

"Do you know what size she is?" Summer asked.

"About like this." He held his hand up beside Summer, indicating his mother's height. "Somewhere around there."

They shopped without much direction, wandering from shop to shop as Summer became increasingly desperate to get some clue as to what would make Mrs. Valletti happy. The wrong choice could make Summer a laughingstock. She could become the girl who had bought a pair of sandals for Mrs. Valletti, only to discover that she was an amputee.

It wouldn't be *that* bad, she reassured herself. Surely Sean would mention it if his mother was missing a leg.

But just as bad, from Summer's point of view, was the way Sean insisted on touching her—a little pressure in the small of her back when she went in front of him through a door, a little shoulder-to-shoulder hug, a chin chuck when she said something dumb about football. All of this while she was walking around wearing his shirt, his number and name plastered on her as if she were his private property.

They stopped for lunch at a waterfront place where they ordered fried conch and grouper fingers and ate them on paper plates out in the sun. It could not have been a more conspicuous place.

"How's yours?" he asked.

"Good," she said, her mouth full of food. She was trying to keep her face lowered, avoiding eye contact with passersby while at the same time trying to check each face.

"I like you," Sean said suddenly. "You're different."

"I am?" Summer said, hating herself for the giddy little-girl tone that crept into her voice.

"Yeah. I mean, you're, like, normal and all."

Summer felt a little deflated.

"What I mean is, you're easy to hang out with," he clarified. "You know, like I don't have to be . . . whatever. There's all this pressure sometimes. Being the big football player and driving a cool car and so on. Girls always expect so much out of me."

"I guess that would be true," Summer said.

"Totally. I mean, Liz? Liz Block? She told me she was surprised when I didn't try to do her on the first date. Like she just assumed I was this animal."

Summer choked violently on a piece of fried grouper. She ran to a nearby trash can and hacked it up with a seriously disgusting noise. When she returned to the table, between the gagging and the humiliation, she could tell her face was a brilliant shade of red.

"Sorry," she said.

"No prob," he said. "You didn't get anything on my shirt, right?"

Summer checked. "No, I don't think so."

"It would be okay even if you did," Sean said generously. "I've had blood all over it, anyway. Football gets kind of violent."

Summer tried out a nonchalant smile. Nonchalant, as if she weren't replaying every second of her gagging-and-choking routine. As if she weren't replaying what Sean had said that had led to her gagging and choking. She had the definite feeling that she was out of her usual milieu, that Sean Valletti, while he might be no older than she, was moving in a completely different circle.

"See? That's what I mean by your being cool," Sean said. "You didn't get all grossed out when I was talking about blood."

"I guess we're even, then," Summer said. "You didn't get all grossed out when I blew fish out of my nose."

He stared at her, and the furious blush that had just begun to recede came back like a flood tide.

Blew fish out of my nose? Blew fish out of my nose?

Then he smiled. "Yep, I like you. I can't wait till we get back to school in the fall. It'll be like, 'What? You're going with Summer Smith?' And then you'll come in, only you'll look totally different. You know, the way you look now."

This was confusing. He liked the way she looked now. But he didn't like the way she usually

144

looked. Not that she cared, she reminded herself, suddenly remembering with a flash of intense guilt that the only guy whose opinion she cared about was Seth.

"Do I look different than I usually do?" Well, it couldn't hurt to ask.

"Duh," he said. "Back home you're always wearing all these big, floppy things, and scarves and coats and all, and glasses."

"I don't wear glasses," she said.

"Really? Huh. I thought you wore glasses."

"No."

"Anyway, you just need to dress more like this," he said.

"I can't exactly wear a bathing suit and a football jersey to class," Summer pointed out.

Sean smiled. "It would be kind of cold. All I know is, I saw you here, and you were this totally different girl. You're all tan and you look really hot. You don't mind if I say that, do you? I mean, about looking hot. Because you do."

"Thanks. Probably deep down inside I'm still the same humble, average girl, though," she said, with the first sarcasm she had shown toward him. He did not notice.

Sean laughed. "Who cares? You and I will be the coolest-looking couple at this big party, this Bachelorama."

"The Bacchanal." Okay, so Diana was right. He was not a genius.

"Bacchanal. Party. Whatever, right?"

Summer tapped her foot against her chair distractedly. "Actually, Sean, I'm not sure about that. I–I kind of already told this other guy I'd go with him."

Sean didn't try to hide his surprise. "What guy?"

"This guy I met down here," Summer said, gazing at her plate of fish.

"Can you call it off?" Sean asked. It sounded more like an order than a question. "I mean, seriously. What's the point of a little summer fling, when you and I have something that could last?"

Summer couldn't even respond. Sean didn't strike her as the most astute guy in the world, but it was almost as if he'd read her mind.

He reached across the table and took her hand. "Please? This whole summer has changed for me since I found you—"

He pulled her around the table and onto his lap. Summer resisted, but not with any sincerity.

He kissed her.

He was not a bad kisser.

"Because I feel like a total creep. I feel like something that would get stuck on the bottom of your shoe if you walked through a gas station bathroom. I feel like a criminal. Like someone should track me down and arrest me and throw me into jail and beat me with sticks." Summer made a face that expressed total self-loathing, absolute disgust with herself.

Diana just grinned. "Arrest you? Who would that be? The Love Police?" She laughed her dry, not-quite-sincere laugh.

"It isn't funny." Summer threw herself on Diana's bed and curled up in a ball. "I have to hide somewhere. I can't let Seth find me yet. I would just blurt out everything. I can't believe I let him kiss me. I am such scum."

"Ah, self-loathing," Diana said brightly. "You've come to the right place. I know all about feeling like scum. But you chose the wrong place to hide out. I mean, there's still one TV truck camped out in the driveway."

"I thought there were six," Summer said.

Diana shrugged. "I guess the others went off after some other story. I heard some supermodel freaked out and shot her husband. Anyway, I guess that's a bigger deal than poor little Ross Merrick, who couldn't quite . . . anyway."

The phone rang. Summer jumped.

"If that's Seth, I'm not here!"

Diana picked it up, listened, arched an eyebrow. "Diana. Who else would it be?" She listened some more. "Yeah, Summer is here. . . . Uh-huh. Yeah, she's all upset because she let that guy with the hairy chest kiss her."

Summer leaped up off the bed and menaced Diana with her fist. "If that's Seth . . ."

"Relax. It's Marquez." Into the phone she said, "Come on over, then. Just tell the TV guy you're our maid."

147

Marquez arrived twenty minutes later, looking disgruntled and cranky. Once again Summer wondered if Diana and Marquez had somehow switched personalities.

"The TV guy isn't there anymore," Marquez told Diana.

"No one?" Diana seemed surprised.

"He was driving off just as I came up," Marquez said, "tearing out of here so fast I thought maybe he found out about, you know, how you feed on human souls."

"Maybe he just got a look at that blouse," Diana said, sneering at Marquez's outfit.

"So," Marquez said to Summer. "Tonsil hockey with the big dumb guy from Bonzoburg."

"Bloomington," Summer corrected automatically. "And it was mostly him doing it."

Marquez winked at Diana. "Mostly," she repeated.

"I just keep thinking, what if Seth had walked by right then?" Summer said.

"Yes, that would have been bad," Marquez agreed. "Although maybe it would do him good. You know, guys get so arrogant when they think you like them. It never hurts to put them in their place a little."

"I don't *want* to put Seth in his place," Summer wailed.

"So then what's the deal?" Diana asked. "Why are you going out with Sean and *mostly* letting him kiss you?"

Summer shrugged. "You guys wouldn't understand."

Marquez clapped her hands together briskly. "Yeah, you're right. So now what should we talk about?"

Summer ignored her. "Look, Sean Valletti is *the* cool guy at our school."

"It's a sad little school, isn't it?" Marquez said.

"You don't think he's cute?" Summer demanded.

"Cute? Sure, he's cute," Marquez said. "Big deal. Cute is fine. But look, even I don't think cute is everything. I mean, if cute was all anyone cared about, we'd all three be going after Diver, since he is undeniably the cutest guy on planet earth." She paused and in a deeper voice added, "Totally cute." Then, as if snapping out of a momentary trance, "But look, as cute as he is, there was nothing there. You know."

"Just because when *you* kissed him he ran screaming for the nearest exit," Diana said.

"That's not exactly how it happened," Marquez said sharply. "Although . . . close enough," she admitted.

Diana just smiled, a smug, faraway expression that intrigued Summer.

"My point is," Marquez continued, "that just being cute or popular is not everything. And I'm shocked that you, Summer, of all people, would be affected by such superficial considerations."

Diana agreed. "Yes, I always thought of you as deep and sort of moral, you know?"

149

Marquez put her arm around Diana's shoulders, and the two of them slowly shook their heads at Summer. "Your mother and I are very disappointed in you, Summer," Marquez said solemnly.

"Yeah, right," Summer said. "You can't say anything, Marquez. You're the one who taught me that relationships shouldn't mess up your life. That's why you were chasing Diver, because you kept saying how nice and low-stress it would be, no heavy emotional stuff like with J.T. Plus you were the one telling me about the end of summer, how Seth would go off one way and I'd go off the other, and I'd be devastated."

"You took romantic advice from Marquez?" Diana asked, rolling her eyes.

Marquez winced. "Look, forget all that. Okay? Do you like this Sean guy?"

Summer sighed. "Actually, it was kind of a surprise. He's this major cute guy, and every girl is all hot for him. But it turns out he's kind of a jerk."

"Kind of a jerk?" Diana said.

"Kind of a jerk in the way that Bloomington is kind of cold in January," Summer clarified.

"And how do you feel about Seth?" Marquez asked.

"I'm totally in love. Like I get these warm flashes every time I think about kissing him. Like when I think about *not* seeing him, I feel sick to my stomach."

Marquez actually smiled. "Well, then, duh. Even you can figure this out."

"But summer's going to end. How can I stay with him when I know that it's going to be really painful?"

"I guess if you love someone that much, you have to accept the fact that it can end up being painful," Marquez said solemnly.

"I do *not* believe I'm hearing that come out of your mouth, Marquez," Diana said. "If that's true, then why aren't you going with J.T. anymore?"

Marquez looked mightily uncomfortable. "Oh, that. Did I mention that we're back together?"

Summer and Diana just stared at her.

"It's no big deal," Marquez said. "It's not like it's happily-ever-after time."

Suddenly there was a light tapping sound at the glass door of Diana's balcony.

Summer jumped. Marquez cursed. Diana smiled.

"Call the cops," Marquez hissed. "This is the second floor!"

But Diana opened the door. The shock when Diver stepped inside was total. At least it was for Summer and Marquez.

"I didn't want to ring the doorbell," he offered by way of explanation.

"That's okay," Diana said. "You don't have to worry about my mom."

Diver looked down at the ground. He usually seemed rather serious, but now he seemed several stages past serious. His mouth was grim, his eyes uncharacteristically evasive.

151

"I, um, thought I'd better come tell you, before someone else told you," he said to Diana.

"What?" she asked sharply.

"Out in the bay. The harbor patrol is out there. They're fishing out a body."

"Someone drowned?" Marquez asked.

Diver nodded. He kept his attention focused on Diana. "I was out there, and a guy I know came by in his boat. He told me who it was. I didn't want you to hear about it on TV or something. It's Ross Merrick. The harbor patrol say it was an accident. Ross is dead."

They watched from Summer's deck, the deck where Diver spent most nights sleeping. The sky was clear and the stars were out, blazing gloriously overhead.

Brighter, though, was the searchlight of the harbor patrol boat, making an artificial noon out of a few square meters of black water. Other small craft had clustered around—the curious, anxious to find out what was going on. And on one of those boats Diana watched a second bright light appear—the light of a television camera.

The body of Ross Merrick had already been dragged aboard the harbor patrol launch, but they weren't leaving yet. Everyone was hanging around in hopes of being on TV, Diana thought cynically. Or, to be grim, they were looking for some kind of evidence associated with Ross's death.

Diana, Summer, Marquez, and Diver watched as

a boat left from the dock of the Merrick estate. It sped toward the scene, slowing as it neared. Two silhouettes were visible: Diana had little doubt who they were: Adam and his father. Adam, going to identify his dead brother. The senator, going to view the remains of his eldest son.

Diana turned away, unnoticed by the others. She sat on the far edge of the deck, looking back toward her own home, so reassuringly bright in the night. Her own bedroom window, glittering through the branches of the trees.

It was odd, she thought, watching the way emotions boiled up within her, watching herself as if she were really up there on her balcony looking down at this sad little spectacle.

It was hard to sort out any one single emotion. The first, instant reaction had been pity. For Adam, mostly. She had loved Adam once. And Adam had never been all bad. Not even mostly bad. He was just loyal to his brother and, more important, loyal to his father.

She even felt a small share of pity for Ross. Nothing he had done—not even what he had tried to do—deserved death. She supposed he had been drunk, as he usually was. Probably while out in the Merrick boat, recklessly high, he'd fallen overboard.

However he had died, it was a shame. Ross had deserved to go to jail. He had needed to get some help. He had not deserved to end up facedown in the bay with his lungs full of warm salt water.

Diana shuddered at the image. These gentle,

familiar waters would never again seem so benign.

There was another emotion too. It struggled with the decent emotions of pity and concern. It was dark and evil, and yet it pushed its way to the surface of her mind repeatedly. Triumph. Not joy exactly, but a cruel, animalistic sense of triumph. Ross had been made to pay for his assault on her. He had paid. He would never again threaten her or any other woman.

Diana noticed that her leg was pressed against a small, metal box with a hinged lid. It was battered and rusty, and had been shoved under an overhang of the eaves.

She opened it, idly curious. Inside were things she recognized—the clothing that she and Summer and Marquez had bought for Diver. It brought a faint smile to her lips. The store tags were still on every item.

She lifted the clothing, and underneath saw more things, junk mostly. A key chain in the shape of a tiny buoy; a cheap disposable razor; a bar of soap; a small, tattered book of poetry; bits of string and Band-Aids and a chewed-up ball.

"Diana?"

Summer's voice. Diana quickly dropped the lid on the box.

"Diana? Are you okay?" Summer came and sat beside her.

Diana tried to still her emotions. She didn't want to betray anything to the others. They would understand pity. They would never understand, or forgive, those darker feelings.

"Sure," Diana said. "I just didn't want to watch anymore."

"I understand," Summer said. "This wasn't your fault. You know that, right?"

"Yeah, it was probably because Ross got drunk," she said. "He drank a lot, even before all this."

"Exactly."

"I didn't want this to happen," Diana said.

"Of course you didn't," Summer agreed.

"I mean, no, *really*," Diana insisted, as if Summer had argued. "No way did I want this to happen. I was mad, sure. I did try to get him to . . . to deal with what he'd done. I mean, I'm sorry. I even said I was sorry that his father got dragged into it and that it had to become this whole scandal, with TV and everything."

"Diana, listen to me," Summer said. "This is *not* your fault."

Why did Summer keep saying that? Diana wondered angrily. Of course it wasn't her fault. She didn't kill Ross, for heaven's sake. She had just been trying to get him to admit . . . to deal . . . to . . .

"I wanted to hurt him," Diana whispered.

Summer said nothing. Behind her, Diana could feel Marquez and Diver watching her silently.

"I wanted revenge," Diana said softly. "I wanted him to suffer. I wanted them all to suffer. That's what I wanted. I . . . I guess . . ." She couldn't talk anymore. Her throat had closed up, and her stomach felt as if it might heave at any moment.

"Got to go," she said through gritted teeth.

She slithered and scraped her way down to the walkway and ran blindly toward the house.

"I have to go after her," Summer said.

"No, leave her alone," Diver said.

"But she's hurting, Diver," Summer protested. "I know what she's thinking. I know what she's feeling."

Diver smiled crookedly. "No, you don't, Summer," he said gently. "I do. Let her be alone."

13

Anyway, Jennifer, those are all the exciting times here on beautiful Crab Claw Key. Diana has turned back into Diana—withdrawn and snippy and antisocial. I've tried to talk to her a couple of times over the last few days, but as usual, she isn't easy to get close to. Diver just says to leave her alone. For some reason he's now the expert on Diana. The cops have dropped the whole thing because no one really sees any point in investigating. The senator says he's going to resign. I guess you saw that on TV. He looked sad.

Marquez and J.T. are back together, which means they're always either having these screaming fights or else they're making out.

The four of us, me and Seth and J.T. and Marquez, went out as a group the other night. It was kind of cool, because obviously I love Seth, and

I really like hanging out with Marquez, and J.T. and I have this relationship . . . I don't know, it's kind of hard to define, really. I guess it's a little like brother and sister. He teases me and I tease him back, but we also feel kind of close. Maybe I'm starting to get adjusted to the fact that he really might be related to me. I guess now I kind of hope he is, because despite the fact that he's temperamental and can get into these really deep low points, he's mostly funny and sweet.

Maybe you'll get to meet him. You know, if. And if, and if, and if. And if! My entire life is one big if. I wish I could be sure of just one thing. Is J.T. Jonathan? Are Seth and I going to stay together? What about the fact that I can practically *see* the end of summer coming?

Fortunately Sean Valletti has been off on his uncle's boat. They went up to Miami for some stupid reason, and I think by the time he gets back he will have totally forgotten I even exist.

I know, that *does* sound strange, doesn't it? It used to be I thought it would be the greatest thing in the world if Sean even noticed me. Now I hope he gets over me.

But you *know* how I drive all the men wild with desire.

I really hope Seth never finds out. It was just this stupid flirtation because I used to have a crush on Sean. Really immature of me, I know.

Anyway, tomorrow is the Bacchanal, the big street party. Marquez totally *lives* for this thing. I got the night off, so I'm going. Seth, naturally, hates the whole thing. Seth isn't exactly Mr. Wild-Dance-in-the-Streets, but he says he'll meet me there, for part of the time at least.

I wish you could be there, Jen. I miss you. Things get so weird around here sometimes. It would be nice to have someone around who knows me the way I really am. For some reason I've been thinking a lot about home lately. I'm not exactly homesick, but it's as if this vacation has gotten bigger and more important than I ever thought it would be. It was supposed to just be . . . like punctuation. A period at the end of the sentence. Then on to the next sentence.

But somehow it has changed everything. What if J.T. really *is* Jonathan? My life back home won't be my old life back home anymore. And then there's Seth. Like I said, it's all ifs.

I would really like at least one thing to be for sure. It's eating at me, grinding my nerves, wearing me down. I wish J.T. would just *do* something to get an answer. Anything. And as for Seth and me . . .

When I left home to come here I was this person who'd never had a serious boyfriend. I'd had crushes on guys—duh, Sean Valletti for one—but actually being in love is a whole new level. A crush . . . well, there's no pain in a crush. But if you really love someone, there's always the possibility of getting hurt, this feeling like you have no defenses.

I'm scared of summer ending, Jen. Every time I kiss Seth, every time he kisses me, every time I even just look at him, I get this little jab, this little voice saying, "It won't last, Summer. It's almost over." I feel as if I've gotten so much older in just the short time I've been here. My dad used to lecture me to think about consequences, right? "Actions have consequences, young lady." Well, I guess Daddy would be happy now, because all I think about is consequences. All I think about is, how many more times will I be with Seth? How many more times will he kiss me before the last time?

Somehow this is all Marquez's fault. I haven't figured out how or why, but I have to blame someone.

Or else it's the fault of that tarot card lady. She told me I would meet three guys. Why didn't she tell me I wouldn't get to keep even one?

14

The Idyllic Interlude Seems to Be Coming to an End.

Summer walked to work. It wasn't as dramatic as going by Jet Ski, but this way she arrived dry and with her uniform unwrinkled. And now that the TV truck had disappeared from Diana's driveway, there was no reason not to walk. Aside from the fact that at ten A.M. it was already blisteringly hot.

Heat waves shimmered up from the pavement. The sun aimed a laser beam right at her head, completely unobstructed by any cloud. Even for Florida in midsummer it was hot. Back in Minnesota, people baked cookies in ovens that weren't this hot.

The sight of Seth's battered, sagging pickup truck, rattling and shimmying down the road, was welcome. He stopped and leaned out of the window.

"So. Looking for a ride, young lady?"

"No, I like to be at least medium rare by the time I get to work," Summer said. She walked around the truck and climbed in.

"Mmm," Seth said, leering outrageously. "I like a woman in uniform."

"Seth, I am really hot and sweaty," Summer said.

Just the same he leaned across and kissed her. And just the same she let him. Again. And again. And despite the heat they were soon completely lost to the normal world.

"I have to get to work," Summer gasped.

"Me too," Seth said. "I have to meet my grandfather on the job site."

"Marquez will cover for me if I'm a little late," Summer said.

"My grandfather's always late," Seth said.

They kissed again. Summer slipped her hand under his shirt, enjoying the warm, taut feel of his stomach and chest, the smooth skin, the way she could feel his heart beat. It was one of her favorite things, touching him that way. It had replaced Oreos on her list of favorite things.

A horn blared loudly and continuously.

They separated. Summer looked out of the back window. Diana in her little Neon.

Diana pulled around to Summer's side and rolled down her window. "You do know this is a road, right?" Diana asked. "Like people might want to drive on it?"

"Sorry," Seth said. "We were stalled. Couldn't get into third gear."

Diana rolled her eyes and drove away. Seth started down the road after her.

"Third gear, huh?" Summer said.

"That's not to say I wasn't enjoying second gear an awful lot," he said.

They arrived quickly at the restaurant. Summer straightened her uniform and checked her hair in the mirror. "Now my lips are swollen."

"You look perfect," Seth said.

"I look like a girl who's been making out in an un-air-conditioned truck."

"I love you," he said. He said it at least once a day, but suddenly it made Summer angry.

"Do you?" she asked bitterly. "For how much longer?"

Seth looked at her warily. He seemed unsure whether this sudden mood change was serious or some kind of unfathomable joke. "Look, Seth, I love you too," Summer said miserably, her anger already evaporated. "But it's like I'm living in fear. I know that sounds dramatic and all, but I can't help this feeling. It's . . . dread. That's the word. Between J.T. and you, I don't feel sure of anything anymore."

He put his arm around her, and for a moment she enjoyed his embrace, but then she pushed him away. "See? That's it, right there, the way I feel. Like I love it every time you touch me, and right behind that comes this fear, and I think no, push him away, keep him away, because the closer he gets the more it will hurt later."

"Look, Summer, somehow we're going to work everything out," Seth said.

"Really?"

"Yes. Absolutely."

"How?"

He stared at her, and then looked down at the floor.

Summer sighed. "I have to get to work," she said heavily.

"Summer, I love you," he said again, "and the end of summer vacation won't change that."

"I love you too," she said, touching his cheek. "But I have to go."

"Look, um, this is probably not the time to mention this, but I may not make it to the Bacch." He seemed to flinch in anticipation. "My grandfather has this rush job, and we may end up working late tomorrow night."

"Oh," Summer said. She bit her lip. Then she smiled crookedly. "Kind of a preview of the end of summer, huh?"

He looked miserable. "We're still on for diving this afternoon, right?"

She wanted to say no, just to give him a taste of his own medicine. But she could not deliberately push him away. At least not yet. "Yes, of course," she said. "Gotta go."

She climbed out of the truck, went around to the back door of the restaurant, and ran smack into Marquez and J.T. They were making out, leaning against the whitewashed back wall of the restaurant.

"I can't believe you two," Summer said with mock disgust. "Making out in this heat?" She was doing her best to shake off the tears of frustration that threatened to fill her eyes.

"Oh, Summer," J.T. said, seeming flustered. A meaningful look went between him and Marquez.

"J.T. wants to ask you something," Marquez said.

He smiled ruefully. "Yeah, I kind of do," he said.

"So?" Summer said.

"Look," J.T. began, "it's this whole thing. I realized that it's just kind of eating away at me. Not knowing."

"Yeah, not knowing does kind of chew your nerves," Summer agreed, way too strongly. Should she tell him about her call to the hospital in Minnesota? No. They hadn't promised to send her the footprint, and even if they did, would it really prove anything?

"Anyway, what I was thinking was, maybe I should just ask my parents outright, you know?" J.T. said.

Summer nodded. She felt a wave of relief. Yes, he should just ask his parents. That was the answer. Then at least she'd have one answer. "If you feel you can do that, J.T., I think it would be a good idea."

"Now you're getting to the fun part," Marquez warned under her breath.

"I can't just blurt it out," J.T. said. "I mean, you

can see that, right? It's like accusing them of . . . I don't even know. If I'm Jonathan, then they could be kidnappers or something." He shook his head in bewilderment. "It sounds insane even to say it."

"Yeah, so J.T.'s concept of a sane way to handle it is for all of us to go over to his house together," Marquez explained, "and we'll do a little barbecue—"

"I'll cook and everything," J.T. said.

"—and we'll tell them the story about Jonathan," Marquez said, watching Summer for a reaction. "And see if they totally lose it."

"Oh," Summer said. She took several deep breaths. She liked the idea of J.T. finding out. The idea that she had to be involved too . . . she liked that idea a lot less.

"Like Hamlet," J.T. offered helpfully. "You know, where he tricks his stepfather by reenacting the—"

"No," Summer interrupted. "You two are crazy."

"It could be a little intense," Marquez said.

But J.T. wasn't laughing. "Summer, I have to know. Sooner or later."

"I understand," she said.

"I tried to convince him later was a better way to go," Marquez interjected.

"And you would go along with this?" Summer asked Marquez. "You? What happened to avoiding other people's potentially horrible personal messes?"

"I'm still hoping to break a leg before then," Marquez said. "I don't even like barbecue."

"Will you do it?" J.T. asked Summer, pleading with his eyes.

"Well, you may be my brother," Summer said, trying to make a joke of it. "So I guess I have to. But even if you weren't, you'd still be my friend. I guess the answer is yes. When?"

"Tomorrow. Right before the Bacchanal gets going. A little backyard barbecue," J.T. said.

"Barbecue and intense family psychodrama," Marquez said. "Please, someone kill me before then."

Several hours later, Summer was underwater. The last time she had gone scuba diving with Seth, things hadn't worked out so well. But they had made a solemn vow since then to leave cave diving off the agenda.

They glided over the coral, careful not to break any of the fragile protrusions. The sun was still high in the sky at four in the afternoon, and it sent down rays that were like individual searchlights, each seemingly adjusted to highlight a particularly beautiful bit of coral or brighten a passing fish. Summer passed her hand through a beam, actually feeling the warmth of it though they were twenty feet down. She exhaled and watched the turmoil of bubbles roil up through the light, diamonds floating toward the surface.

It was an incredible place, as alien as anything

could be while still being part of planet earth. A hundred species of fish darted by, alone or in schools, some on urgent errands, some just floating along, droopy-lipped and sad-eyed like the grouper that seemed to be watching them. Maybe he was bummed that Summer had eaten one of his relatives with Sean.

The coral was mostly white, but with fantastic extrusions in pink and blue. It served as home to crabs and snails and eels and things whose names she didn't know. Unfortunately, it was also home to more divers than Summer could keep track of—some with tanks, some snorkeling, dropping down from the surface for as long as their air lasted, then kicking hard for the surface.

Oh, well, their last dive had been private. Far too private. She would try not to resent the fact that the reef was as crowded as a supermarket at rush hour.

Seth tapped her shoulder and pointed to the surface. They began their slow ascent, never rising faster than the tiniest of their bubbles.

They broke the surface. It was always a sort of mystical experience for Summer as she passed through the barrier between one world and another. She pulled off her face mask.

"Hey, what are all those great big fish that look exactly like us?" she asked Seth.

"It is kind of crowded down there, isn't it?" he said.

"But totally beautiful," Summer said. "Thanks for bringing me."

They swam to their small motorboat and climbed in heavily. Summer lay sideways on the bottom of the boat, exhausted. Seth slithered in beside her. They both laughed.

"I'm much, much heavier up here in the air," Summer said. She shrugged out of her tank, grateful for the freedom of movement. "I have regulator lips," she said, laughing some more. Her lips often felt a little numb and rubbery after being wrapped for an hour around the regulator mouthpiece.

"I can fix that," Seth said. He kissed her. His lips were as cold as hers.

After a while they separated and lay side by side, Seth's chest cushioning Summer's head. The sun had slipped toward the horizon, but although it was low enough not to be in their eyes, the sky was still a bright blue, with only a solitary cotton puff of cloud.

"Now I'm hot again," Summer said.

"You're always hot," Seth said.

"Oh, don't you sound like—" She stopped herself just in time. She had been about to say Sean Valletti.

"Sound like who?" he asked.

"Um, like this guy on TV whose name I can't remember," she temporized. Another opportunity to tell Seth about Sean. Another chance to confess her relatively minor sin. But she said nothing. And Seth—trusting Seth—let it go.

"This is nice, huh?" he said. He stroked her hair, which was already drying in the blow-dryer-hot breeze.

"This is perfect," she agreed. And it was—the boat rocking gently on the water, the cries of gulls, the sight of a pelican, that prehistoric relic, swooping majestically overhead. "The sky is never this blue back home."

"No. I guess it has to do with how far south you are. It's a paler blue up there."

"And cold," she said.

"Definitely colder," he said.

"I don't want this to end," Summer said. "This summer, I mean. Marquez, Diana, Diver, J.T. . . . you. It's like the sky. Like everything in my old life will be paler and colder than here. There's no one like Marquez in Bloomington."

"There's no one like Marquez anywhere," Seth said, chuckling.

Summer was annoyed. Obviously she was trying to bring up the subject of her and Seth, not Marquez. "I just don't want it to end," she repeated.

He shrugged. "Everything ends eventually. I guess that's what makes summer so intense, this feeling that it lasts for only a short while and then it's back to reality."

"So you're saying things that are cool for summer vacation wouldn't be so good the rest of the time?"

"Maybe so," he said.

Summer sat up abruptly, breaking the physical contact.

"What's the matter?" Seth asked.

"Nothing," Summer said sullenly. "We should get back."

Seth looked mystified, but he started the outboard engine and aimed the boat back toward Crab Claw Key. It was a thirty-minute trip, and the first half of it passed in silence.

"Hey, is this about the end of summer again?" Seth asked, sounding as if it were a crazy question.

"I'll take 'Doctor Duh' for two hundred dollars, please," Summer said sarcastically.

"I thought we already talked about it this morning," Seth pointed out.

"Yes, but we didn't decide anything."

"Summer, what can we decide? You know how I feel about you. What can I say?"

Summer glared at him. "So you don't even think about it? You don't even care that when summer does end, you go one way, and I go another way, and that's it?"

"What do you mean, that's it?" Seth was beginning to look troubled.

It was a small victory, but Summer was relieved to see that he wasn't totally obtuse. Could it really be that he was just now getting it?

"I mean, I'm in Bloomington, you're in Eau Claire. Me in one place, you in another place. As opposed to now, when we're together in the same place."

"Well, jeez, it's not even a hundred miles, and it's highway the whole way," Seth said.

"Oh, right. So in January when it's two degrees

and the snow is falling, you'll be driving over from Eau Claire a hundred miles to take me to the homecoming dance?" Her sudden outburst of sarcasm shocked them both.

"I . . . I, uh, don't have a car," Seth admitted. "Yet."

"You don't have a car? Neither do I. Then how—"

They stared at each other until Seth looked away to steer the boat toward Crab Claw Key.

Summer felt deflated. Somehow, despite her worrying, she'd believed that Seth would have some ready answer to give her. Some reassurance, if only she continued to press him. But he had nothing. He was just denying the problem existed.

"Look, all we can do is try to work it out," Seth said, kicking at a life jacket that was in his way.

Summer turned away and looked at the island. She could just make out the silhouette of the stilt house, dark against the bright water and the pastel waterfront homes. Her home—for now.

Somehow it will work out, she told herself. She couldn't see how, but it would. It was not possible to believe that fate had brought her here to find Jonathan, only to make her lose her love. Somehow it would all work out.

15

Little Boys, Big Boys, and Brothers

Much later that night, late enough that it was really the next day, Summer found herself in a different boat, alone, it seemed. Sails billowed overhead, red from the setting sun. The sun was already low, bisected by the horizon, and Summer willed the boat onward, chasing the sun as it set in the south.

The sun doesn't set in the south, she told herself. It's a dream. Oh.

Pale blue storm clouds chased her, scudding across the water with frightening speed, as in a time-lapse film, racing clouds like horses galloping down from the north.

A new boat was there, pushed along by the clouds, skimming toward her. Standing in the bow was a small boy dressed all in white.

The little boy's boat was fast. And then he was

173

with her, on her boat, or she was on his, and he was standing, his bare feet—had his feet always been bare?—not quite touching the deck, as if he were floating there.

"Where's the ball? The red ball?" Summer asked.

"I still have it," he said.

"Are you a ghost? You must be dead if you're a ghost."

He smiled. "I'm a memory."

"But I don't remember you," Summer said. "You were already gone when I was born."

Then they were no longer on the boat. They were in the living room of Summer's home in Bloomington, and her mother, her belly hugely swollen, was lying back on the couch (the awful old couch they'd had back then) while the little boy sat beside her and solemnly placed his hands on her stomach, feeling the movements of the baby inside.

A chill went through Summer. This was the closest she and Jonathan had ever come to each other.

"Are you dead, Jonathan?" Summer asked. Now he was standing in the grassy field, preparing to throw the red ball.

He threw it. It landed, bounced sluggishly, and rolled to the fence. The unseen man waited there.

"Jonathan?" Summer said. "Are you Jonathan?"

And then they were back on the boat, racing toward a dwindling sun, the clouds over them turning the sails dark gray.

"Who are you?" Summer demanded, her voice rising to a scream. "Who are you?"

But the little boy in white floated upward, arms outstretched, till he was as high as the top of the mast. Then, with a cry of perfect joy, he plummeted, sliced into the water like an arrow, and disappeared.

In the instant before he struck the water and disappeared, Summer had seen him change. His body was no longer the body of a small child, but of a young man.

She woke crying, sobbing uncontrollably. It had been a dream full of loss and sorrow, and her sleeping mind was unprepared for the onslaught of emotion. None of her defenses had been up.

She had lost Jonathan. She had never even known him, but he had dominated so much of her life with her parents—all the times she had come upon her mother crying silently in some darkened room; all the times she had found her father staring blankly into space, eyes filled with tears of guilt and sorrow. Grief for the loss of Jonathan had always been there, hidden by her parents to the best of their ability, but there all the more for being unspoken.

Summer had grown up dreading that grief, and yet never really feeling that it would touch her. Now grief came in a new guise—Seth. And she was walking toward it, unable to stop herself, heading toward loss and sadness.

Her parents had not known they would lose

Jonathan. She knew she would lose Seth. Was it inevitable? Was there some quota of sadness that had to be dealt to every person? Was that just the way love worked? Because that was the underlying problem—without love, there could be no real pain. Love contained within it the seeds of loss and bitterness and grief.

She had known that. She'd known it, and had always kept her distance, but, trapped in the cave with Seth, when it had seemed the future was not going to be much of a problem, she had forgotten. She had let herself say the words to Seth. Let herself feel the words.

And now she was trapped. She loved someone she would lose.

Summer got out of bed and dried her tears, feeling cried out for the moment. She twisted her baby-tee around the right way and went to the door. She opened it silently, anxious to see a world outside of her dreams.

The sky was already gray in the east, and the stars had already retreated toward the west. She stepped out onto the deck. It was no more than eighty degrees, practically cold, with humidity like steam.

"Hi," Diver said.

Summer was not surprised by his voice. He was above her on his deck, sitting in a lotus position, facing the east. She had long since accepted the strangeness of his sleeping out here, alone, uncovered.

"I hope I didn't wake Frank up," Summer said,

nodding toward the pelican, who sat perched with his ridiculous beak tucked down low.

"No. He woke up earlier," Diver said. "We heard you crying. In your sleep."

"Oh. Sorry. I guess I was having bad dreams."

"Come on," he said. He gave her a hand up the ladder. She sat beside him. The horizon was showing just the first trace of pink.

"You know this *wa* thing you talk about?" Summer said. "This inner peace?"

"Yes."

"Mine is shot totally. Blown up. Destroyed. I have no inner peace," Summer said. "I have no balance."

Diver nodded. "Me neither."

"You too?" Summer asked, surprised.

"Yes. For the same reason." He watched the horizon glumly.

"Love?"

"Yes."

"Diana?"

He sighed. "Yes."

"So how is she? Diana?"

He shrugged. "I hope she'll be okay," he said uncertainly.

"She feels bad, doesn't she? Like she was to blame for Ross?"

"It's complicated," he said cryptically.

"Everything is," Summer agreed. She smiled sadly. "It's a bad idea, this whole love thing. Totally disturbs your *wa*."

"Yep."

The sun appeared, a fiery yellow eye peeking over the rim of the earth. "I usually love sunrise," Summer said. Maybe it was just the lingering sadness of the dream, but the rising sun seemed more ominous than welcome. "The start of a new day and all."

Diver nodded. He seemed to be in tune with her mood. "Not every new day is good."

"I have to do this thing today," Summer said, thinking of her promise to go to J.T.'s. "It's something I want and don't want at the same time. Like hope and fear all in one."

Diver nodded. "Well, I guess every day is like that. Hope and fear."

Summer smiled. He was only pretending to pay attention. His thoughts were somewhere else entirely. With Diana, Summer supposed. At one time she would have been almost jealous. Now she was actually pleased.

"Every day may be like that," she said, "but somehow I think this one is going to be a little more intense than usual."

Across the bay, on the balcony of his downtown apartment, J.T. sat watching the same sunrise, having spent a nearly sleepless night. He had fallen asleep for an hour, perhaps a little longer, but then had been awakened by odd, disturbing dreams.

"Jeez, no wonder," he muttered, taking a swig from a stale beer. He never remembered his dreams, but it was not surprising that he would have them, not with the day he was anticipating. It wouldn't have been surprising if he'd had screaming nightmares.

He tilted the bottle up and drained it. He made a face and shook his head. "Yuck."

He went back inside, grimly sure that he would never get back to sleep. If he got back into bed, it would just mean more of the same—playing scenes over and over in his head. Scenes he'd already played a million times.

He remembered the day he'd cut himself at work and had been taken to the emergency room. He'd been bleeding pretty dramatically, and the doctor had thought he might need a transfusion. He was blood-typed. A passably rare type. Fortunately his parents had been in the waiting room by then. The doctor had pulled their medical records, which were on file.

J.T. remembered the look on the doctor's face. "Oh, you're adopted," he'd said. Why had he said that? Because the blood types didn't make any sense otherwise.

Only, J.T. had never been told he was adopted.

He had tried to get a birth certificate. He had tried to find an adoption certificate. Neither existed.

J.T. got a new beer from his little refrigerator. And then Marquez had told him Summer's story. About the brother who had disappeared sixteen years ago, just when Summer herself was being born. Jonathan, who would be the same age as J.T.

Blue-eyed, blond-haired Summer. Blue-eyed, blond-haired J.T. And, Marquez had said, she'd noticed times when J.T. and Summer seemed to feel the same thing at the same time, to say the same thing at precisely the same moment.

Probably just a coincidence.

Or else some strange fate.

He should try to sleep. He really should. In just a few hours, too few hours, he would try to learn the truth once and forever.

Who was he? Who were his parents?

No, sleep wasn't likely.

J.T.'s parents' home was over on the "new side" of the key, just a few blocks from the gate of the Merrick estate, on one of the canal-front blocks of nearly identical pastel tract homes. It was the sort of place where backyard barbecues were to be found almost any evening.

Summer arrived with Marquez in tow. And "in tow" was the right phrase. At the last minute, Marquez had tried to weasel out of it, coming up with a series of increasingly desperate excuses, including a sudden conversion to Judaism or Islam or any other religion that would forbid her to eat barbecued ribs.

"You're going," Summer had said firmly. "You promised J.T. Besides, you've been to his folks' house before, so you know the way. It'll be fun."

"I could draw you a map," Marquez offered.

But in the end, they had shown up in Marquez's parents' big old sedan.

The first introduction to J.T.'s mother was a shock. Summer took one look at her and wondered how J.T. could have failed to suspect long ago that this woman was not his natural mother. She was short, with dark salt-and-pepper hair drawn back in a bun. She was cheerful and greeted Marquez with a big hug. Summer shook her hand.

"Call me Janet, okay?"

She didn't look like some horrible kidnapper, Summer thought. If she was the sort of person who would steal someone else's child, she hid it well under a disguise of middle-aged normalcy.

J.T. was in the backyard with his father, already tending a pile of glowing coals. J.T. waved as the two girls arrived. He managed a smile, but it was a sickly, nervous grimace.

His father was a second surprise for Summer. He looked so much like his son, they could almost be . . . well, father and son. The same tall, thin body, the same blue eyes, so much like Summer's own. Only, J.T.'s father had brown hair.

Summer tried to remember her genetics lessons from school. Was it possible for two parents with brown hair to have a child with blond hair like J.T.'s? It had something to do with dominants and recessives, but how that applied in this case, she couldn't recall.

"This is my dad," J.T. said, accenting the word *dad*.

"Everyone calls me Chess," he said.

Janet and Chess, Summer noted. Not exactly

the textbook picture of deranged kidnappers. Suddenly the whole thing seemed utterly preposterous. What in the world was she doing there? Marquez was absolutely right. This was beyond nuts. This was a whole new level of bizarre.

Why had it not penetrated her mind what this might involve? So, Janet, Chess, are you kidnappers? Did you steal my brother?

She felt an edge of panic, which was not helped much by the fact that J.T. was grinning like a skull and giggling half hysterically at anything that even sounded as if it might be a joke.

"Oh, yeah," Marquez said under her breath, "this will be fun. How did I let you two talk me into this?"

"My son the cook is handling the barbecue duties tonight," Chess said. "Can I get you girls a drink? Iced tea? Soda?"

"Soda would be fine," Summer said.

"Me too," Marquez agreed. Then, after J.T.'s father had ambled off in search of beverages, she added, "Also perhaps some Valium, you know, just to make this evening at all tolerable."

"Thanks for coming," J.T. said, sounding way too sincere. "I wasn't sure you'd make it, Marquez."

"Summer said it would be fun," Marquez said, giving J.T. a discreet kiss.

J.T. just looked grimmer still. "I don't know about fun. I'm . . . I don't know, I'm feeling like this is insane. Do you think this is just nuts?" He directed the question at Summer.

"No, J.T.," she assured him. "I mean, look, you want to know. I want to know too."

"One way or the other," J.T. said, "I'm not letting anything bad happen to my folks. I don't care what they did sixteen years ago. They're my folks. They'll always be my folks. There are lots of reasons—I mean, maybe it wasn't like that at all. Maybe it was someone else who took me, and they just adopted me, not knowing."

"They seem awfully nice," Summer said.

"They *are* nice," J.T. said, too fiercely. "Sorry. I'm kind of jumpy. I'm a wreck. I scarcely got any sleep at all."

"I understand," Summer said. J.T.'s nervousness was definitely catching. Was that a sign of some kind of brother–sister psychic link between them? If so, then Marquez must be related too, because she looked ready to crawl out of her skin.

"I'm not going to wait," J.T. said suddenly. "Everyone's here. I can't stand here cooking ribs as if nothing is going on."

Marquez muttered a woeful curse.

J.T.'s parents were heading back toward them. Chess carried two sweating glasses of soda. Janet had a plate of what looked like some kind of finger food.

"Mom. Dad," J.T. said. He looked as if he were about to go into shock.

"What?" Janet said. She peered at him in concern.

"We have to talk. All of us."

"I . . . I can't do this," Marquez said suddenly. "I . . . look, I just remembered, I have to be at this place. This, um, place where I have to go."

She turned and almost ran from the yard.

Summer had to fight an urge to go after her. J.T. looked stricken but determined. "That's okay," he said stiffly.

"J.T., what is going on?" his father asked. "Are you and Maria having some kind of a fight?"

"Maybe we should sit," J.T. said, still rigid as a board. He marched over to the picnic table and sat. After a moment's hesitation and an exchange of worried looks, his parents went over too.

I'm going to kill Marquez, Summer decided. But the truth was, this really wasn't about Marquez. With a horrible, sinking feeling, she sat down with the others.

"Mom. Dad," J.T. began again. "I'm eighteen years old. I have a job. I have my own place." It was a prepared speech, and it sounded like one. "I'm an adult. And I think I have a right to know the truth. About me. About who I am."

Summer expected them to act shocked or puzzled or to ask him what he was talking about. Instead Janet just seemed to crumple a little. Her husband slowly lowered his face into his hands.

For a while no one spoke. Then J.T.'s father said, "Summer, I think this is sort of one of those family-only moments—"

"Summer *is* family," J.T. said.

His father raised an eyebrow and looked troubled.

"Tell them, Summer," J.T. commanded, still stiff and formal.

"I don't think—" Summer began.

"Summer is my sister," J.T. said.

"She's what?" Janet said.

"My sister. She . . ." J.T. took a deep breath. "She had a brother named Jonathan. I think . . . we both think . . . that I *am* Jonathan."

"Jonathan disappeared sixteen years ago," Summer said. "We never . . . no one ever found . . ."

Summer waited for Janet to cry out her confession. But to her surprise, J.T.'s mother just reached over and put her hand gently on Summer's arm.

"I'm terribly sorry for you," she said. "I can only imagine what your parents must have gone through all these years." She turned to J.T. "But sweetheart, you are not Summer's brother."

16

*Diana Turns a Corner, but
Summer Falls Off the Edge.*

Diana stood under the eaves of Summer's stilt house and called his name. No answer. She hadn't really expected Diver to be there. It was early yet, though darkness had fallen. From downtown the music and mayhem of the Bacchanal drifted across the water.

"Diver!" she yelled one last time. No answer. He wasn't there.

Diana couldn't wait any longer. She ran up the lawn and around the side of the main house, then tumbled into her car and started the engine.

Maybe he was downtown. At the Bacch. Or else at the marina, where he did odd jobs. But did she have time to try to find him in the crowds? No. The call from the institute had been for her, anyway, not Diver. It was her fault, all her fault, not Diver's.

Still, as the headlights pierced the darkness of the road, she wished he were with her.

She soon encountered the outer edge of the Bacchanal, parked cars lining the road on both sides, reducing it to a single lane. People were everywhere, streaming toward downtown, laughing, playing, some in fantastic homemade costumes, many already half drunk.

Diana honked the horn, but the people blocking her way took it as a joke. They raised a bottle of champagne in her direction, a toast.

Then he was there. Standing just to the side, as if he'd been waiting for her. Like a commuter, waiting for his ride to work.

Diana pulled up next to him. "I need you," she said.

Diver climbed in beside her.

"It's Lanessa," Diana said tersely. "They called from the institute. She's having some kind of breakdown. She won't stop crying. I have to go there."

"I'll go with you," Diver said.

"It's my fault," Diana said. They were deep in the revelers now, crawling along at a frustrating pace through a sprawling party. Masked faces peered into the car. Crude, good-natured invitations were shouted.

"It isn't your fault," Diver said.

"It is," Diana insisted. "I've never missed a day when I was supposed to go. I didn't go today, and Lanessa expected me. I didn't go." She chewed her thumbnail viciously and beat on the steering wheel. "This stupid party!"

"Diana—"

"Get out of my way, or I swear I'll run you down!" Diana yelled out of her window.

The crowd parted enough to let the car through. Diver fell silent. Diana sped toward the highway on-ramp.

The highway was an eerie driving experience, even though Diana was used to it. The dark, nearly empty ribbon of road leaped across vast tracts of water, touching down briefly at a bright point of land before leaping into the darkness again.

"The whole year, I never missed my day at the institute," Diana said. "Even when I was really depressed, even when I was thinking I was going to kill myself, I always made it. Lots of weeks that was the only reason I didn't swallow a bunch of pills. I knew I had to go because there were these kids, and they were so much more screwed up than I was."

"More screwed up than you," Diver echoed, nodding thoughtfully and looking out the window.

"I guess I always figured helping them would help me. I mean, it was selfish, really. That's why I never told anyone else about it. I didn't want people thinking I was trying to be some kind of plaster saint, when I knew I was just doing it for myself."

"So why didn't you go today?"

"I don't know. I've been feeling . . . ever since Ross died. I don't know."

"Lost," Diver said.

Diana stared at him. She nodded slowly.

"Like you don't know who you are anymore," Diver said. He was still gazing off into the dark night. "You used to have a meaning. Hating Ross. Hating Adam."

"Hating myself is more like it," Diana said bitterly.

"Kind of the same thing," Diver said.

Diana turned off the highway, shooting down the off-ramp at twice the speed limit. The institute was dark but for a few muted lights behind shaded windows. The cars of the overnight staff were parked in a little knot to one side, clustered under a streetlight for safety.

The housemother led Diana and Diver straight to Lanessa. "She started about five hours ago, just sobbing," she said. "All she would say was that she had been bad. Then we figured out she was distraught because you hadn't come today. I think she feels she's being punished." It was not an accusation, but Diana didn't need any help to feel terrible.

They found Lanessa in her room, curled up with her thumb in her mouth. She was convulsing with dry sobs.

Diana rushed to her and lifted the little girl's head onto her lap. "I'm sorry, Lanessa, I'm so, so sorry."

But Lanessa didn't react.

"Come on, Lanessa, I'm sorry I didn't come today. I . . . I don't know what happened. I just wasn't feeling right, I guess. Come on, honey, come on." She stroked the little girl's hair. "Did you think I didn't like you anymore? Is that it?"

Lanessa shook her head.

"Did you think I was mad at you?" No response. "That's it, isn't it? You thought I was angry at you?"

Finally Lanessa nodded.

"Sweetheart, I wasn't angry at you. Not at all. I could never be angry at you." Diana remembered the details of Lanessa's case. For Lanessa, having someone angry at her had not just been a reason to pout. Anger had been followed by terror and pain. An adult's anger had nearly killed her.

"Lanessa, I was angry, but not at you," Diana said. "I was just mad at the world, and all these different things. But not at you."

"I don't think she understands the difference," Diver said. "The people who hurt her, they were just mad at the world too. Just like the people who hurt you, Diana."

"And you?" Diana said to him.

"Yes," he said tersely.

"So what am I supposed to do?" Diana asked him. "What's *she* supposed to do?" she continued, stroking the child's head.

"I don't know," he admitted. He looked troubled, agitated, uncertain.

"And here I thought you were all-wise," Diana said sarcastically. She could feel Lanessa pulling away from her. "Lanessa, no, it's all right, this doesn't have anything to do with you."

"Of course it does," Diver nearly shouted. Diana was stunned. She had never seen Diver upset. It didn't even seem possible that he could shout.

"Of course it has to do with her," Diver said more quietly. "It has to do with everyone. Everyone gets hurt. Everyone has bad things happen to them, and then everyone wants to hurt those who hurt them. Till pretty soon every single person on earth is either being hurt or hurting someone else. It's insane."

"So what's your brilliant solution?" Diana demanded. "You want us all to forgive and forget? You think Lanessa should maybe just forgive her parents for what they did? That's what you want?"

"No," Diver said. "I want the people who hurt Lanessa to burn in hell, that's what I want. And the ones who hurt you, and the ones who hurt me. That's what I want." He clenched his fist in the air, as if choking a person visible only to him. "I want them to cry. I want to see them suffer."

Diana shrank away, shielding Lanessa with her arms. But Lanessa was not afraid. She was watching Diver with bright, glittering eyes.

He took several deep breaths. "But I figured out after a while that I couldn't spend my life punishing everyone who deserved to be punished."

"So you just forgive them?" Diana said.

He shrugged. "I guess so. Not because they deserve to be forgiven. They don't. It's just that when you go around hating people and wanting to hurt them . . . You just can't do that. That isn't life. You forgive so you can live." He sat down on the bed, rested his head in his hands, and stared at some remembered scene only he could see.

After a while Diana said, "I didn't know you could talk that much, Diver."

"I don't usually," he said, a little sheepish.

"You know what I've been feeling for the last couple of days?" Diana asked him. "I've been mad because Ross died. I was angry because he escaped, in a way, before I could hurt him."

Diver nodded. "Been there."

For a while none of them said anything. Even Lanessa was quiet, her sobbing stilled. "Can we go see Jerry?" she asked at last.

"Oh, sweetheart, Jerry is asleep now," Diana said. "We should let him sleep."

"No, he's up," Diver said wearily. "He'd like to see Lanessa. As a matter of fact, he's waiting in the tank for us to go see him. He thinks maybe Lanessa would like to see him catch his Frisbee."

Diana smiled at him. "Diver, you may be very smart about certain things—smarter than I am—but you *cannot* really communicate with animals."

Diver laughed. "Of course I know I can't communicate with animals, Diana. I'm not crazy."

Naturally, when they arrived at the tank, Jerry was up. He was waiting patiently by the side, amusing himself by tossing a Frisbee up in the air, as Diana was not really very surprised to see.

✶   ✶   ✶

J.T. was not Jonathan. That single fact occupied Summer's entire mind. J.T. was not Jonathan.

The little boy in her dreams really was dead. The brother she had never met, but whose tragedy had shadowed her entire life, was not suddenly going to turn up in a big, happily-ever-after ending.

She had left J.T. at his parents' house, the three of them crying and laughing and retelling the story of how J.T. had come to be suspicious, and the story of why J.T. was not the biological child of his parents.

Summer had been crying too, but for different reasons. She left with a gaping feeling of loneliness, no longer anything like a part of their lives, and had walked back into town. She never had gotten any barbecue. But the Bacchanal had opened its arms to greet her, drawing her into the crowds, squeezing her in, carrying her along in the shrill high spirits.

Someone handed her a paper cup, and she drank its contents without thinking. Some kind of punch. She winced at the sweetness.

J.T. was not her brother. She was surprised by how much it disturbed her. She hadn't ever really absorbed the possibility that he might be, until suddenly he wasn't. She told herself this was good, that she hadn't wanted to believe, because if J.T. had been Jonathan, then all the laws of probability had to be rewritten, and the impossible would have been possible, and miracles would have popped up in the fabric of ordinary life.

No, that wasn't true. She *had* wanted to believe.

She'd wanted to believe in miraculous happy endings. She wanted to believe in improbable things . . . that long-lost brothers would be found, that true loves would not be lost at the end of the summer.

And yet J.T. was not her brother. And Seth was not even here. He was off working with his grandfather. Just a taste of the endless stream of excuses she could expect in the future, after they each went to their separate homes. He would be in Eau Claire. She would be in Bloomington. How many times would they make dates and then break them because something had come up? Sorry, Summer, I know I said I would come, but the weather . . . this job I have to do . . . this exam I have to study for . . . I can't borrow the car. . . .

In the back of her mind, Summer knew she was being unfair. Seth wasn't like that. If Seth said he would do something, he could be relied on.

"Yeah," she muttered darkly, "like I could rely on him to be here tonight."

The crowd carried her toward music, two live bands pounding out competing covers of everything from salsa to punk, all at terrific volume. Everyone was dancing, and, without meaning to, so was Summer, rising and falling as dictated by the crush of bodies. A feeling of dizziness crept over her.

Then she saw Marquez atop a bench, dancing with someone Summer didn't know, someone Marquez probably didn't know, either. Her brown curls were flying. Her face was beaded with sweat.

Summer pushed her way through the crowd, ignoring various calls of "Hey, baby" and "Come on, dance with me." She grabbed Marquez's shorts by the pocket and yanked.

Marquez looked down, annoyed, then, recognizing Summer, gave her a rueful smile. She climbed down.

"You mad at me?" Marquez yelled in Summer's ear.

"What, for leaving me when you swore you wouldn't?" Summer said sarcastically. "Why would I be mad?"

"Don't be," Marquez pleaded. "Come on, it's the Bacch. Party and forget it."

"He's not Jonathan," Summer said.

This got Marquez's attention. She looked concerned. "He's okay, right?"

"Do you care?"

"Jeez, Summer, look, I never said I was good at this stuff. I don't deal with people's problems very well, all right? So I'm selfish. So I'm superficial. I don't care. I had to get out of there. I couldn't just sit there and watch. Either way it was going to be bad. If he *was* Jonathan, then probably J.T. would have lost the only family he's known. If he wasn't, then you . . . your brother was . . ."

Summer nodded. "Yeah, I know," she said, her eyes filling with tears again. "I guess I had started to buy into it. I mean, what if? What if Jonathan never died? Wouldn't it be the greatest thing on earth to be able to go to my parents and say, guess what? Your son didn't die in a gutter somewhere. He wasn't killed. Here he is! He's alive! No more sadness. Happy days are here again." There was more bitterness in her own voice than she had ever heard there before. "The world basically sucks, have I ever mentioned that?"

"No, and I can't believe you're saying it. Where's Seth?"

"He is working. He's working, and I'm here, and he's not, and I think that paints a pretty clear picture of my future with Seth," Summer said.

Marquez began to look uncomfortable. "Okay, well, then let's just dance and flirt with guys and forget all this stuff," she said. "Forget it all."

Summer grabbed her friend's arm. She knew Marquez wanted her to shut up and stop being so grim, but she didn't care. She felt desperate and sad. "I was going to go back to Bloomington in triumph. I mean, when I left I was just any other girl. But I was going to go back and say to my parents, hey, I found Jonathan. And at school I'd be one of those girls who's all sure of herself and above it all because I was in love with this great guy. And now you know what? It'll be like, yeah, I went to Crab Claw Key, and all I got was a tan. After a week that will fade, and I'll be right back to being the same old Summer Smith."

"Summer! There you are!"

Summer heard the voice but took a few seconds to recognize it. Sean. She managed to turn, elbowing a nearby reveler in the stomach.

Sean was right there. The crowd surged and

threw her against him. He put his arms around her.

"Hey, I'm back," he announced.

"Yeah, I see."

"Back from Miami. Man, what a dump that place is. This is so cool! These people know how to party! Let's try to get something like this started back home."

Summer almost remarked sarcastically that it might be a little different throwing a street party in a place where everyone had to wear parkas instead of bathing suits. But she didn't. "Yeah, when we get home" was all she said.

"Here!" Sean handed her another cup of punch.

"Thanks," she said, taking a sip. In spite of the strange dizziness closing in on her, she didn't stop to think about what exactly was in the punch.

He kissed her, and she let him.

She felt sick and strange and irritated. Too many things to worry about. All of it stupid and pointless. It didn't matter, any of it. Marquez had the right idea—dance and party, and whenever anything serious threatened to rear up in your face, run away.

Summer looked around for Marquez, but she had been swallowed up in the crowd. So she danced with Sean and finished her second glass of punch, and let him kiss her and kissed him back, and stopped caring about everyone and everything. It was all going to come to an end, all of it: Seth, and J.T., and Marquez, and Diver. But mostly Seth.

She felt as if someone had stabbed a knife into her stomach and twisted it. Seth. He wasn't even there with her. And already the feeling of emptiness was so intense. She should never have let it happen. She should have kept him away, at arm's length. Then she would have been safe.

Sean drew her close. She felt strangely numb. Sean was holding her tight against him. She knew she should pull away, but she couldn't seem to summon up the energy. What was the point?

Then she saw him. Seth. He was staring at her.

"Seth," she whispered. He *had* come. Her heart leaped.

For a moment her view of him was blocked, and he was gone. As he would soon be gone from her life.

Sean grabbed her and kissed her again, pulling her against him. Seth reappeared, but now it was only a momentary glimpse as he turned away.

17

Terrible Truths: Sean Valletti's a Jerk, and Maria Marquez Is a Sweetheart

As a rule, Summer did not drink. Once or twice she'd had a single beer. Which was probably why she hadn't thought much about the sickly sweet taste of the punch. Which was probably why the weird dizziness hadn't clued her in about its alcohol content. Now that she'd spilled her third glass down the front of her blouse, she should have been worried, but instead she found it terribly funny.

In fact, everything was funny. The way she was walking. The way her words weren't coming out right. The way Sean was propelling her down the street away from the Bacchanal, half dragging and half carrying her.

"Is this the right way?" he demanded.

"What?"

"Is this the right way to your house?"

"My house? Why are we going there?" Summer asked. She tried to focus, but couldn't quite.

"Why do you think?" Sean said.

Summer didn't know the answer, but she had the feeling she should. "I want to go back to the party."

"We're moving the party to your place," Sean said. "Have a real party."

"I don't know." Suddenly she was very tired. She sat down on the curb too quickly, bruising her behind in the process.

Sean took her hand and tried to pull her to her feet. But Summer offered no help, and after a few tugs Sean gave up. He sagged to the ground beside her. A passing car honked and gave a jeer.

"I think I may be kind of drunk," Summer said.

"No kidding," he said. "That punch was spiked with grain alcohol."

"I'm sleepy."

"You can't sleep here," he said. "I'll take you home. You can sleep there. Or at least you can go to bed." He laughed uproariously.

Summer leaned close. He tried to kiss her, but she fended him off. She had something important to say. If only she could remember what it was. Oh, yeah. "You know, everyone thinks you're really cool. At school and all."

He grinned. "Yeah, I know."

She whispered into his ear. "Did you know I used to have dreams about you? You and me?"

"Tell me about them," he said. He kissed her and then trailed kisses down her neck.

"Now I dream about this little boy. The little ball boy."

"Yeah? Forget that. Tell me what you dream about me."

Summer realized that he had slipped his hand up under the back of her blouse. "What?" she said, squinting against a pair of headlights.

"Dreams. Tell me about them."

"Oh, anyway, like I said . . . um . . . everyone thinks you're really cool."

"Hey, and if you're with me, everyone will think you're cool too," he said.

"Who?"

"Everyone," he said.

"What?"

He became impatient. "I said, if you're with me, everyone will think you're cool too, all right? Come on, let's get back to your place." He dragged her upward with more determination this time, and she staggered against him. "Then I'll show you *why* all the girls think I'm the best."

Summer began to giggle. She pushed him away, laughing loudly. "You're such a jerk."

"What did you call me?"

"I don't care," Summer said. "Because, like . . . I mean, it doesn't matter. One way or the other, Seth and me . . . he goes boom, over that way, and I go the other way."

"Who is Seth?"

"Boy number three," Summer said, suddenly sad in a way that momentarily sobered her a little. "See, the tarot lady said guy one, he's dangerous, right? Well, that was Adam. And the mystery guy was number two, and that's Diver. And boy number three, the right one. That was Seth."

"Did you call me a jerk?"

"She didn't tell me that he was only temporary. Did I say that right? Tem-po-ra-ry. She didn't say, oh, by the way, you'll fall in love, but then it will be over. Like Jonathan, you know. Love someone, and then they go, and all you have is . . ." She started to cry, but at the same time she was laughing. "Then all you have is Sean Valletti."

Sean retreated in horror. "Wait a minute. You're only with me because this other guy dumped you?"

"He did *not* dump me," Summer said, offended.

"You, Summer Smith, are with me, Sean Valletti, because some other guy *might* dump you? Like I'm some kind of . . . of . . ." He was so outraged he couldn't speak. "Who is this guy? Are you telling me he's better-looking than *me?* Are you trying to tell me he kisses better than *me?* Who do you think you are?"

Summer leaned against a lamppost and considered going to sleep.

"Oh, man," Sean raved. "I told my sister I was going with you. She's probably told everyone by now. Okay, look, let me just make one thing clear here. I'm dumping *you*. All right? Listen to me! I am officially dumping you, so don't even think about telling anyone that you blew me off, because that would be a total lie."

"What?" Summer said.

"That does it. You are on your own," Sean said. He turned on his heel and disappeared back in the direction of town.

Summer used the lamppost to lever herself to her feet. Where was she? Not far from downtown. Maybe she could go and sleep in the restaurant. Home was way, way too far.

Then she saw a house she recognized. Just half a block down the street. She could make it that far.

Marquez paced a circle, staring all the while at the floor of her room, the area in front of the counter. Yes, it was time to start it. It would be a totally new challenge. She would have to paint it from the center out, otherwise she'd leave footprints, and that would ruin everything.

She could see the picture in her mind, the way it would grow over time, till it met up with the walls and everything came together as one vast mural.

She heard the pounding on her window, insistent, persistent. It had been going on for a while, she knew, maybe as long as half an hour, maybe more. But she wasn't going to react. She'd removed the extra key from its hiding place.

The floor would be an aerial scene. First the Bacchanal as if you were looking at it from above, all those dancing, gyrating, partying bodies. She'd paint that first, then over that paint a framework, and it would look as if you were walking on a glass floor, looking down through it at the town. Perspective, that would be the challenge.

The pounding at the window continued, varying in rhythm, each shift distracting her just a little.

"What?" she suddenly yelled. She stomped to the door and threw it open. "What? What? What?"

J.T. smiled, as if he had not been standing there pounding till his knuckles were raw. "Oh, hi, Marquez," he said. "Can I come in?" He stepped past her without waiting for an answer. He noted the paints lined up ready on the counter, and noted the fact that she had cleared everything off a large part of the floor.

"What do you want?" Marquez demanded.

"I just came by to see you," he said.

"Well, I'm busy."

"Doing the floor, huh? Good. It's about time. I knew you'd be painting," he said smugly.

Marquez calmed herself enough to talk reasonably. "J.T., look, I'm sorry I ran out on you and Summer. Okay? Now can you just leave?"

"Yeah, I knew you'd be painting," he said. "You always do when you get upset. Or when you're hurt. Or even when someone you love is hurting."

"Don't psychoanalyze me, J.T. You're the one with the messed-up head."

"True, true," he said equably. "Although I'm feeling a lot clearer now. How about you?"

"I'm fine. Thanks for asking. I'll see you at work

tomorrow. Afterward I'll do whatever you want. Just go away now."

"I love you, Marquez," he said.

This tack unsettled her a little. "I know. You said that the other night."

"And you love me," he said.

"Okay, so everything is happy, happy, joy, joy," Marquez said. "I love you. Now go away."

Instead he sat on the edge of her bed. "It wasn't what any of us thought," he began. "I was right about my parents not being my parents. About not having a birth certificate around anywhere, just a baptismal paper from when I was two."

Marquez fretted impatiently. She really wanted to be painting now. And J.T. was just distracting her.

"But all the reasons I'd worked out were wrong," he said. "I'm not Jonathan. I'm not some little kid who was kidnapped."

To Marquez's surprise, he started to leave.

"Where are you going?" she asked.

"Why do you care?" he said coyly.

"Look, just tell me the stupid story. You started it, now finish it."

"I don't know, Marquez," he said dryly. "It's got all these emotional parts, people getting hurt, people with problems. Like me. Complications. You wouldn't want to have to feel any of that, would you?"

"Fine, then go," she said. "No, wait. Listen to me, J.T., you think you have me all figured out, but you're wrong. I have a right to decide stuff for myself. I have a right to stay away from people who are going to drag me down, because I don't want to be dragged down. Go talk to Diana—she gets off on being depressed. I don't. I'm not an emotional person. What is that, a crime?"

J.T. just laughed. "You're not an emotional person? Marquez, you are so pathetic. You're the most emotional person I know. You feel everything, that's your problem. You *feel* and then you can't stand it, so you run away. You run away and put it all up there, on the wall. You didn't run away from my parents' house today because you're some coldhearted, unfeeling person. A person like that wouldn't have minded a little family tragedy. That's why I wasn't mad at you. That's why I knew you'd be here, trying to get it all out of your head and your heart and put it on the walls, where it would be safe."

"Oh, yeah?" Marquez said, unable to think up any better comeback.

"Yeah."

"That's a bunch of crap," Marquez said without conviction. She sat down on the bed, and J.T. moved beside her.

"You're right," J.T. said kindly. "Just a bunch of crap. But don't worry, I won't tell anyone that underneath it all you're a warm, sweet, generous person who really cares about her friends."

Marquez shuddered. "You're making me sick."

J.T. kissed her hand. "You want to hear the rest?"

Marquez sighed dramatically. "Like I have a choice?"

"It was my dad's sister. She was my mother."

"Excuse me?"

"She got pregnant—no one is exactly sure who the father was, or is. Anyway, my dad's sister got pregnant. But when I was being born, there were problems. She died in childbirth." J.T. shook his head in wonder. "She died *because* of childbirth. My folks didn't want me growing up with that kind of burden. I knew my dad had a sister who died, but I never knew she was my biological mother. That's why they never had a birth certificate around—it would have shown my real mother's name. Then I would have known, and I guess I would have grown up feeling as if I had been responsible for my mother's death." He gave her a rueful smile. "You think I'm messed up now? Just imagine how messed up I might have been."

"I don't know," Marquez said. "It might have been good. If you were even more messed up, I might have gotten the floor painted before now. So . . ." Her face grew sad. "So Summer's brother really is dead."

"Or at least he isn't me," J.T. said. "She tried to hide it, but I think she was kind of upset."

"She was," Marquez agreed. "I saw her at the Bacch. She was drinking punch."

"Summer? Drinking?"

"She was bummed. So naturally I took off," Marquez said unhappily.

J.T. squeezed her hand. "She'll be okay. Know how you're not as tough as you think you are? Well, she's tougher than everyone thinks she is."

18

Only a Miracle Can Cure a Hangover.

Summer woke very suddenly.

She opened her eyes. She was in the stilt house, in her own bed. Her head hurt. Her eyes hurt. Her mouth was dry and gluey. Everything around her was buzzing. Her stomach . . .

She jumped up, cried out in pain, and raced for the bathroom. She spent several minutes on her knees in overly close contact with her toilet.

When she got up at last, she was trembling, her knees were shaky, and she was feeling rotten and filthy and disgusting. The face in the mirror made her groan.

"How did I get here?" she wondered.

She remembered the lamppost. She remembered telling Sean Valletti something . . . she couldn't recall the exact word, but he hadn't liked it, she was sure of that.

Then she remembered Seth. The way he had seen her kissing Sean. The look in his eyes.

She threw up some more. Afterward she took a shower and brushed her teeth twice, gulping water as if she'd been in the desert for a week.

"Why do people drink?" she muttered. "This isn't fun. This isn't even anything like fun. This is the worst feeling in the world." What a total idiot she was for gulping down two glasses of that disgusting pink punch without even thinking about what was in it.

Her first thought was that she had to find Seth. And then the other memories began to trickle back into her mind. A dark jerky vision of herself staggering up a walkway, banging at a door, and collapsing.

Seth's house.

"Oh, no," she moaned.

He had brought her here. She vaguely recalled being in his truck. In the back. He had dumped her in the back of his truck. Like garbage or something.

He had carried her down here.

And someone . . . *someone* had gotten her out of the clothes she'd been wearing and into the boxers and baby-tee she wore to bed.

"Please, just let me die," she said. It would be a relief from the endless explosions going off inside her head.

There was an obscenely loud banging noise at her door.

She grabbed her head and went over to open the

door. Sunlight hit her with physical force that sent her reeling back, shielding her eyes and crying aloud.

"That's the same reaction I had to your outfit, Marquez," Diana said.

"It was you she saw first," Marquez said. The two of them came in and, much to Summer's relief, closed the door behind them.

"Not hung over, are you?" Marquez asked Summer.

"Shut up," Summer growled.

"I think Summer may have been drinking," Marquez said, laughing.

"No kidding. I was the one who had to change her clothes last night," Diana said.

"You? Oh, man, thank you," Summer said.

"Me and Seth and Diver and these three guys we met," Diana said. Then, seeing Summer's look of horror, she relented. "Just me, it was just me. Your chastity and purity are intact. Seth came and got me to help."

"Seth brought me here? After . . . after what happened last night?"

Diana's eyes darkened. "Yes, because Seth is a truly decent guy. You stab him through the heart, and he picks you up off the floor."

"He's upset?"

"No, why would he be?" Diana said sarcastically. "Just because he sees you swallowing half of that guy's face?"

Summer felt the urge to throw up again. She

struggled to get it under control. "I was upset," she said.

"Did you trade Seth for that muscle-boy dweeb from Birdbrainburg?" Marquez said, making a disgusted face. "I guess you decided you really liked the hairy chest, huh?"

"You don't understand," Summer said. "I love Seth."

"Oh, *now* I understand," Marquez said. "That clears it up for me."

"You're the one who told me, Marquez—the end of summer. What about the end of summer? What am I supposed to do, just get closer and closer to Seth? Fall more and more in love, and then *wham* . . . Ohhh." She grabbed her head in pain. "Look, I don't live here. This isn't my real life. You two aren't even real. Reality is Bloomington. That's where I live. That's my life. And I don't want to be there and go to bed every night crying because . . ." A sob escaped from her, but she was too dehydrated for tears. She took several deep breaths.

"Summer, all that stuff I said about the end of August—why would you listen to me? You know I'm full of it," Marquez said.

"No, you're not," Summer said. "You were right. I'm sorry if I hurt Seth—"

"Just ripped his heart out, that's all," Diana said in a low voice.

"But it was never going to be for real. It was just a summer thing. And I'm not a person who can be in love for three months and then forget it and move on."

"Summer," Marquez protested, "you don't know for sure what's going to happen when the summer ends."

"I know you guys are trying to be nice," Summer said, "but I have to throw up."

"Okay. We'll, uh, get together later," Marquez said, sounding relieved to have an excuse to leave.

When she was done in the bathroom, Summer drank a lot more water. And thanks to the water, when she began to cry, she was able to shed tears.

She slept most of the day, her hangover gradually easing into a more general depression. She got up only once, to eat a dry sandwich, call in sick at work, and stare blankly at Letterman for a while, surprised that he was on so early, and then slowly realizing that it was almost midnight.

She turned off the TV and lay there in the dark, listening to the sound of the water lapping against the pilings, barely noticing the creaking boards and soft shushing of waves against the shore.

This was as bad as she had ever felt. She still felt sick. Worse by far, she felt heartsick. The thought of Seth hurting, in pain, feeling betrayed and abandoned by her . . . She couldn't stand the images that came into her mind, and yet she couldn't keep them from coming.

It doesn't matter, she told herself. Now or later,

it would have happened just the same. And later it would have hurt even more. Better that Seth just thinks I'm a worthless slut who would go with Sean Valletti. Better to make it quick and final, right now, than to let it drag out, let the dread build up day by day between now and three weeks from now.

She'd been stupid to let it get started. She had wanted to fall in love this summer, thinking that love was just another form of entertaining fun, like scuba diving or sunbathing. Another cool thing to do at the beach. But it wasn't. It was dangerous. Without love you couldn't have pain. Without love you couldn't have loss. Grief. Emptiness. Love made it all possible.

If she had never loved Seth, she would be happy right now. Love. It was just like alcohol. A little fun followed by a long, painful hangover.

"Love is like alcohol," she said, liking the sound of it, as sleep crept over her again. It sounded very deep. It sounded wise. She would get it printed on a T-shirt. No one would understand what it meant.

She dreamed. She was on the plane again, just arriving on Crab Claw Key. The tarot lady was beside her, just the way it had really happened. Only now the lady had turned over a card with a picture of a cup full of punch.

"That's the love card, isn't it?" Summer asked the lady.

"Huh?" the lady said.

"You told me there would be three guys," Summer said. And then she was no longer on the plane, but back in the underwater cave, trapped in the dark with Seth. Seth was sleeping, and then the little boy appeared, dressed all in white. He was holding the red rubber ball.

"You again," Summer said.

"Still here," the little boy said.

"No. You're not," Summer said, feeling a terrible sadness. "You died. You're gone."

The little boy looked at her, his eyes uncertain.

"I'm sorry," Summer said. "You're just a dream."

"Oh, *that*," the boy said dismissively. "Everything is just a dream. So what?"

She closed her eyes, wishing him away, but when she opened them again, they were standing in the grassy field.

"Jonathan, just leave me alone, okay?" Summer pleaded. "I don't like it here."

"I can't. I keep dreaming you," he said.

"No, I'm dreaming *you*," Summer insisted.

"I don't think so. You're sunny. You keep showing up here."

"I'm not sunny, I'm alcohol. No, no, I mean, I'm Summer," she said.

"Don't say that," the little boy said, suddenly frightened. "You're disturbing my *wa*."

There were bright blue numbers. A five. A three. A two. Her clock.

She rubbed her eyes. It was 5:32. In the

morning, she was pretty sure. Yes, it had to be morning. As for which day, who knew?

But she was awake. Awake and no longer sick. Groggy but alive. She would go watch the sunrise with Jonathan. No, with Diver. Go watch the sun come up with . . .

Every hair on Summer's neck stood on end. She stopped breathing. Her skin was tingling, electric. Oh, my God.

In a flash she was outside, out in the clinging predawn damp.

She looked up at him.

He was staring down at her with wide, awe-struck eyes.

In his hand he held something. Without a word, he handed it to her.

Summer cradled it in her two hands. It looked as if it had been chewed by a dog. The rubber was dried and crumbly with age. In the faint, gray light it was impossible to tell its color, and yet Summer knew it had once been red.

"It's the only thing I've kept all these years," he said.

"I . . . I dreamed," Summer said.

"Yes," he said. "Sunny. I didn't know who you were. There are so many things I don't remember. Memories lost except in my dreams . . ."

"Yes. Me too," Summer said, her voice choked.

He bent over and helped draw her up onto the deck.

"Jonathan?" she asked in a whisper.

Diver smiled. "I guess so. I'd forgotten. They gave me another name, but I knew all the time it wasn't right."

"Jonathan," Summer said, definite now. "You're not dead."

"No," Diver agreed. He looked puzzled. "And what was that about you being alcohol? You said it in your sleep."

Summer laughed. She took his hand and held it tight. "That was some dumb idea I had. Back before I realized that there really can be miracles."

"Here she comes," Diver said as the fiery rim of the sun appeared on the horizon.

Summer watched with him for a while as the sun rose and the stars disappeared and the water turned from black to blue.

"I guess it's a good thing we never went out or anything, huh?" she said.

"Speaking of a very disturbed *wa*," he agreed. Then his expression grew troubled. "This means Diana's my cousin."

Summer shook her head. "Diana's mom is my dad's . . . *our* dad's sister." Every nerve in her body seemed to tingle at that thought. "But she was adopted. There's no actual blood relationship."

"Good thing," Diver said, smiling with relief. "That would have been sad."

Summer smiled. She laughed. "No way. Miracles are never sad."

19

Huh Huh, Huh Huh . . . Love Sucks.

It was late morning when Summer at last parted from Diver. He would probably always be Diver to her, she decided.

A Federal Express package had arrived from the hospital in Minnesota. In it were the impossibly tiny footprints of Jonathan Alan Smith, born eighteen years earlier. But it no longer mattered to Summer. She knew the truth now. It was a true miracle, or else fate, or perhaps just a coincidence. That didn't matter either.

Four years earlier, at the age of fourteen, he had run away from the people who had taken him from his home, left behind the name they had given him, tried to leave behind the pain that had been inflicted on him. He had followed the coast, always heading south, begging, stealing, doing odd jobs, learning his way around boats and the water so well that he'd earned the nickname Diver.

From New Brunswick, Canada, where he had started, down to Weymouth, Maine, to Cape Cod, to Ocean City, finally to Crab Claw Key. As if he'd been drawn there, making a four-year trip to a rendezvous.

Or else, Summer thought, it was all just coincidence.

She borrowed Diana's car and drove to Seth's house. She was bursting with excitement. Later she would tell Diana and Marquez, and, soon, her parents. But first she had to go to Seth. She had to tell him: Miracles *do* happen. Maybe she was allowed more than one.

She knocked at the door and experienced a momentary flashback to the night before. No, it was the night before that. She'd staggered here to this door, and Seth had brought her inside, where she had . . .

. . . had thrown up on the kitchen floor.

"Oh, man, I could have lived without remembering *that*," she muttered. She knocked again, steeling herself for his accusing, angry look.

The door opened.

"Oh, hi," she said, taken aback. It was Seth's grandfather. "I, um, I don't know if you remember me," she said. "I'm Summer. I'm a good friend of Seth's."

He looked her up and down, a disparaging look. "Some good friend you are."

"Is Seth home?"

222

"Not yet," Mr. Warner said. "He'll be home in about ten hours. Home in Eau Claire. Poor kid."

"What do you mean, Eau Claire?"

Mr. Warner shrugged. "He left. All of a sudden. He wouldn't even tell me why, but I haven't lived sixty years not to know that there was a female behind it."

Summer was staggered. No, this wasn't what was supposed to happen now. It couldn't be. She couldn't find Jonathan and then lose Seth. Not now. Not now.

"He can't have gone," Summer said in a whisper.

Mr. Warner looked at his watch. "Eleven-oh-five flight. He's gone, all right. And who's gonna help me with my business the rest of the season? That's what I want to know."

Summer looked at her watch. "It's only ten fifty-nine. Your watch is fast." She calculated quickly. Six minutes. No way. She'd get killed trying to make it to the airport in six minutes.

"Bye!" she yelled.

She raced for the car.

It was four minutes after eleven by the time she slammed to a screeching, rubber-burning halt in front of the tiny airport. She leaped out, leaving the door wide open. She had just reached the glass doors of the terminal when she heard the crash.

She spun and saw Diana's Neon, half turned. The door was off, lying in the road in front of a taxicab whose driver was shouting at the top of his lungs.

Summer ran inside. The gates, which way? Left! She ran. The metal detector! No, she couldn't just blow it off, they'd shoot her or something.

With excruciating slowness she was forced to walk through the metal detector. Her purse took an eternity to pass through the X-ray machine.

She looked at her watch. Too late! No, no, it was too late. Still she ran. The sign—Miami. That had to be it, there was always a plane change in Miami.

"I have to get on that plane!" she yelled to the frightened desk clerk.

"It's leaving," the desk clerk said.

"It can't," Summer cried. "I have to get on. It's a matter of . . . of . . . of true love!"

"You're kidding."

"No, please!"

"Well, you can buy a ticket on the plane, just out that door—"

Summer ran. Out the door. Across the burning tarmac. They were beginning to roll back the steps.

"Wait!" She ran up the steps. The mechanics rolled it back into place and she hurtled through the door and stumbled against the flight attendant.

"Welcome aboard," the flight attendant said. "May I see your ticket?"

"I don't have one," Summer said. "The lady back there said I could buy one."

The pilot began taxiing the plane down the runway. The engines revved louder.

"How would you like to pay?"

Summer froze. "Excuse me?"

"The ticket. How would you like to pay? Cash? Credit card?"

"Credit card! My dad gave me a Visa card for emergencies. Good old Dad." She fumbled in her purse and produced the card. Good old Dad was going to kill her. Maybe she could just explain to him that it was a case of true love. Or maybe Diana would kill her first for having wrecked her car.

She caught a glimpse of Seth. The seat next to him was empty.

"Hi," she said, panting and gasping and grinning.

His look of amazement was almost worth the cost of the ticket. She hoped her father would agree.

"What are you doing here?" he demanded angrily. His eyes were red and swollen.

"What am *I* doing here? What are *you* doing here?"

"Going home," he said sullenly.

"Don't, okay?" she pleaded. "Don't go home. Not yet. It's still summer. It's not the end of August yet."

"That doesn't matter," he said grimly. "It's too late. You told me yourself. What's the point? It'll only come to an end, and then we'll both feel worse for having dragged it out."

"When did I say that?"

"The other night. Right before you blew chunks all over my kitchen floor."

Summer sighed. "Look, I know all that. I mean, it's still true. You can't have real pain without real love. You can't feel grief and loss and hurt without love. Love is the only way you can ever be really hurt, deep down. It's all still true."

"So?" he asked.

"So . . . it's also true that you can't ever really be happy without love, and you can't ever feel like . . . like I feel when I'm with you. I like that feeling." She took his hand and held it between both of hers. He did not pull it away. "It's basically just a messed-up situation."

He nodded reluctantly. "Yeah. Love sucks."

"It kind of does," Summer agreed.

"Pretty cool, though, too," he said in a low voice.

"I love you, Seth," she said.

"I love you," he said.

"Can we go now?"

"Um, Summer? We're in the air already," he said.

"Oh. Will you . . . will you kiss me when we get to Miami?" Summer asked.

"No," he said. "I'll kiss you right now."

He did. And she did. And when she opened her eyes she saw a woman sitting across the aisle. A very familiar woman.

The tarot lady winked at her and shuffled her deck of cards.

"Oh, no, you don't," Summer said. "Don't even think about it."

After Katherine Applegate graduated from college, she spent time waiting tables, typing (badly), watering plants, wandering randomly from one place to the next with her boyfriend, and just generally wasting her time. When she grew sufficiently tired of performing brain-dead minimum-wage work, she decided it was time to become a famous writer. Anyway, a writer. Writing proved to be an ideal career choice, as it involved neither physical exertion nor uncomfortable clothing, and required no social skills.

Ms. Applegate has written sixty books under her own name and a variety of pseudonyms. She has no children, is active in no organizations, and has never been invited to address a joint session of Congress. She does, however, have an evil, foot-biting cat named Dick, and she still enjoys wandering randomly from one place to the next with her boyfriend.

For everyone who believes—
a romantic and suspenseful
new trilogy

KISSED BY AN ANGEL

by Elizabeth Chandler

When Ivy loses her boyfriend, Tristan, in a car
accident, she also loses her faith in angels. But
Tristan is now an angel himself, desperately
trying to protect Ivy. Only the power of love can
save her...and set her free to love again.

Volume I
Kissed by an Angel

Volume II
The Power of Love

Volume III
Soulmates
Coming mid-August

Available from Archway Paperbacks
Published by Pocket Books

1110

Summer

by
Katherine Applegate

Three Months. Three Guys.
One Incredible Summer.

June Dreams
51030-4/$3.50

July's Promise
51031-2/$3.50

August Magic
51032-0/$3.50

Simon & Schuster Mail Order
200 Old Tappan Rd., Old Tappan, N.J. 07675
Please send me the audio I have checked above. I am enclosing $_____ (please add $3.95 to cover postage and handling plus your applicable local sales tax). Send check or money order — no cash or C.O.D.'s please. Allow up to six weeks for delivery. You may use VISA/MASTERCARD: card number, expiration date and customer signature must be included.

Name _____

Address _____

City _____ State/Zip _____

VISA/MASTERCARD Card # _____ Exp.Date _____

Signature _____ 1088-02